D1597606

Gianna Mia

Gianna Mia

Virginia J. Marangell

Dodd, Mead & Company · New York

I would like to give special thanks to Rosemary Casey, who gave so much thought and care to the editing of this book.

All characters and events in this book are completely fictitious. Any resemblance to persons living or dead is unintended.

Printed in the United States of America

1 2 3 4 5 6 7 8 9 10

Library of Congress Cataloging in Publication Data

Marangell, Virginia J
Gianna mia.

SUMMARY: The youngest of the Dellesantos chronicles the lives of the family in their Italian community of New Haven from 1937–1953.
[1. Family life—Fiction. 2. Italian Americans—Fiction] I. Title.
PZ7.M326Gi [Fic] 79-52047

For my husband Joe—
who shared the tears, the laughter, and the dreams

Contents

PART I

Of Old Dreams

1937-1938

1

Her reflection gazed back at her from the pastry-shop window, dark eyes solemn, thin arms full of books. She was twelve years old, reaching toward thirteen with an impatience almost unendurable because her birthday was still so far away.

Thirteen was the magical age. Twelve was still a child, weak, dependent, but thirteen was the beginning of womanhood, and she intended to be strong and independent. No one knew yet just how strong and independent she was going to be. They would all be shocked, she thought in secret delight.

Oh, why was time so slow?

Her mother always got angry with her because she wanted to grow up so fast. "Why do you wish your life away? When you are grown-up and married and having a family you will wish you were twelve again."

Zia Louisa also had a few comments. "Be happy to stay as you are," her aunt would say. Then she'd add in that mysterious tone of voice that older women used when they spoke about Life, "You don't know how lucky you are," implying that there were things ahead that were mysterious and undesirable.

Gianna had been to the library and now she waited

for her father to come swinging around the corner of Grand Avenue. Then she would hurry to meet him and he would cry out in delight, "Gianna! Gianna mia!"

Beyond her reflection in the window she saw the huge, dustily beautiful model of St. Peter's Basilica which Nick Perrone, the owner of the pastry shop, had fashioned from sugar. It filled most of the window space, and it had been the wonder of the neighborhood and the city of New Haven two years ago in 1935 when it was new. A photographer from *The New Haven Register* had come to take pictures of it!

Nick had known a brief time of glory. The real miracle of it was that Nick, an immigrant, had never had an art lesson and never seen St. Peter's Basilica.

"It's God," Gianna's mother, Maria, had explained once. "God gives to each person a special talent. And this is Nick's talent."

A man came out of the pastry shop carrying a square white box. A fragrance of anise and confectioners' sugar touched the air, and Gianna's mouth watered, as she thought of the rum cake.

Oh, that delicious rum cake! Layers of delicate sponge cake soaked with rum, and rich vanilla and chocolate cream fillings between, thick whipped cream covering the whole thing, the fancy ruffled edge, and pink and green roses and shiny red writing across the top.

She saw her father in the window and turned to meet him.

Cesare Dellesanto was handsome in the sunlight, big and strong with dark red hair and flashing black eyes. Not movie-star handsome like Clark Gable or Tyrone Power, but earthy, lusty, powerful. Even in his work clothes and construction shoes. He carried his battered tin lunchbox, his jacket slung over his shoulder.

"Hi, Papa!"

"Gianna mia! So you come to meet your old papa, eh?"

With his free arm he reached out and gave her a brief hug. Gianna breathed in his masculine odors of sweat and cigar smoke, and her heart rebelled against the word old. Old meant something on the way out, something that would soon be lost and gone. And she could never think of her father that way.

She walked beside him down the street, past the pastry shop and the fortune-teller's, and the bread bakery. The fresh yeasty smell of new-baked bread caressed the autumn air.

Her father glanced at the books she carried and smiled. "More books. You read them all?"

She smiled. "Of course, Papa."

He looked pleased. "So what kind you get today, eh?"

"I have one you'd like, Papa. It's about some ruins they've discovered near Athens. Do you know, when they dig down they uncover one city on top of another sometimes, each one from a different time period?"

"What's that big book?"

"That's another one on archaeology."

"Why you read those books?"

"Because that's what I want to be, an archaeologist."

He groaned. "Why you can't be teacher or nurse, something useful?"

"Because I want to go on expeditions like I read about in these books. I want to help discover ruins and lost civilizations. Maybe in Italy or Greece. Maybe in Africa."

He laughed then, the idea so preposterous to him that it wasn't worth considering seriously. "You mean—dig? Like they dig ditches?"

She was offended. "Not quite like that, Papa. It's very different."

"But they still dig."

"Ye-es."

"Take my advice. You don't have to go to college to dig ditches. So how was school today? The sister, she give you good marks?"

"I got all A's and 100's today, Papa."

Cesare beamed with pride. "Of course," he said. "Why not? You're Cesare Dellesanto's daughter. What marks could you get? You take after your papa, you remember. My side of the family. Not your mother's side. They don't know nothing."

"Did you get A's in school when you were young, Papa?"

"What you think I am now, a hundred? Make no mistake, your papa's young like a boy still. I get A's? All the time. The teacher, she tell my father, 'Why you send this smart boy to school? He should be teacher, not pupil.' "

"Oh, Papa!"

"So what's for supper tonight?"

"Macaroni."

He grinned. "What kind?"

She stopped to think. "Just plain macaroni."

"So what's a difference? With Mama's tomato sauce it's good enough for a king, eh?" He started to laugh at his own joke. "For a king. Me, I'm the king. Down at the club they call me king."

"Well, you're a king to me, Papa."

Cesare touched her curly black hair and said tenderly, "And you are princess to me, Gianna mia."

They had come to their own street now. Six-family tenements rose up against the sky in dark brick squalor, overshadowing the wooden three-family and single dwellings. Here and there the dreariness was broken by a lone elm tree, leaves tinged with gold.

Down on the corner stood St. Michael's Church, its doors open to the faithful, the symbol of order and hierarchy, the reminder that in the midst of all life's hardships there was a God who loved you and cared what happened to you.

Across from the church was Columbus Park, a grassy square fenced in by wrought iron, with a scattering of elms, and a statue of Columbus looking out at the many funeral parlors of lower Chapel Street.

They passed Zio Luigi's tenement. Gianna looked up curiously at the closed blinds.

Cesare's face darkened. "You don't go there, you understand? Never!"

She didn't ask why. When your father said don't go you didn't go. That was a cardinal rule of life.

She never knew exactly what it was about Zio Luigi that angered Cesare so much, but she was sure her mother's brother had some connection with the underworld. He drove a new Cadillac every year, and Gianna saw him on the street sometimes, swarthily handsome and always beautifully dressed. She would stop to talk to him and he would try to give her money, which she always refused out of respect to her father's wishes.

It was always a temptation to accept her uncle's invitation to have coffee in his house, where a pretty young blonde girl lived with him. She had heard whispers of the luxury inside that tenement, of the thick carpets, the priceless paintings, the exquisite furniture. But of course she would never go.

Other men on the street were also returning from work in their shabby work clothes, carrying their battered tin lunchboxes. They waved to Cesare and called out greetings in Italian, then turned in at their own alleyways.

"Here we are!" Cesare said gaily, his steps suddenly lighter, his eyes a little less weary. "Home from the wars!"

Home from the wars of life, from the bitterly backbreaking daily struggle to put food on the table, pay the interest on the mortgage, and make the monthly payments on the bank loans for the tuition payments for his sons, Julio and Eddy, who were attending college in Boston.

The waning gold of the afternoon sunlight glimmered on the windowpanes of the little gray house so incongruously sandwiched in between the tenements. Coming from a family of landowners, Cesare had struggled, gone hungry, to buy the house before he married. His father's last words to him before he left Bari, Italy, were: "Buy land. Live in your own house when you marry. Whatever else changes in the world, land will always be valuable. Better to live in a one-room shack on your own land than in a mansion that belongs to somebody else."

Gianna hurried alongside her father down the alleyway. In the backyard the fruit trees had lost their greenness. Across the high wooden fence at the end of the yard loomed the brick dress factory, its lights turned off for the day. It was here that Gianna's mother had worked as a seamstress before her marriage.

In the back hall Cesare hung his jacket over a nail and flung open the door to the kitchen, shouting to his wife, Maria, and his two older daughters, Rose and Annamarie, "Throw the macaroni! The king, he's home!"

He grabbed Maria, who was holding a handful of spaghettini, and started to dance with her, humming the music of the tarantella. The three girls laughed gleefully at the sight of Cesare's huge figure bobbing around and Maria reeling unsteadily, her dark eyes flashing with impatience, her braid of gray hair almost coming unpinned.

He let her go so suddenly she almost fell over, the spaghettini perilously close to being dropped on the kitchen floor, and he cautioned her, "Now you be sure to make it *al dente.*"

She gave him a black scowl. "I make you *al dente* if you don't stop this crazy fooling. You're lucky I didn't drop the macaroni."

Cesare looked at his laughing daughters and shrugged his huge shoulders. "You see? Your father, he can always laugh and make jokes, but your mama, she can only be cross. It's her side of the family that's like that. My side, they always laughing and happy."

He pinched Maria's cheek, after she had flung the macaroni into the big pan of boiling water, and even she had to laugh then. "How can you joke after so much hard work?"

"How? Because I'm a king, I'm A-1 boy. And after I eat I go out and work some more so all my children, they can go to college and be something special."

Rose brought out a decanter of wine, made by Cesare and his sons from the Concord grapes in the backyard, and poured some into a glass. Cesare took the wine and went into the living room where, in his own special chair, he lit a fresh cigar and opened the evening paper.

The kitchen became again a woman's world. The spaghettini boiled furiously in the big dented aluminum pot, the tomato sauce simmered on the back of the stove, and a tiny silver crucifix glimmered serenely on the wall, as if to bless all cooking efforts.

While they talked, Gianna wiped the oilcloth on the table and set the places with the dishes, chipped and unmatched, and the forks and knives that had long ago lost most of their silverplate and now had a worn, greenish look. Annamarie grated Parmesan cheese into a bowl, while Rose sliced the big loaf of Italian bread.

Maria tasted a strand of macaroni, considered for a second, then nodded her head in satisfaction. *"Al dente,"* she said to the girls, as she carried the steaming pan to the sink to drain. "Call your father and brother."

The ceiling light shone brightly down on the six of them at the table. Cesare at one end, Maria at the other, Gianna and Annamarie on one side, Rose and the seventeen-year-old Paolo, who had been upstairs, on the other. It was a full table, even without the two missing ones. Eddy, Gianna's favorite brother, hoped to go on to law school in two years. Julio, the most brilliant one in the family, was in his last year of pre-med and eligible for a number of scholarships.

During a lull in the conversation, Gianna looked at Cesare and asked, "Are we poor, Papa?"

He frowned at her. "Why you ask?"

"No reason. I just wondered."

He put down his fork and looked at his family around the table. "No," he said, quite definitely. "Poor is when you got nothing, when you go hungry, when you're all alone. You got nothing?"

"No, Papa."

"You hungry?"

She glanced down at the macaroni steaming in the dark red sauce. "No, Papa."

"You alone?"

"No, Papa."

He waved his hand to dismiss the matter. "Then you're not poor."

Dinner ended, and Paolo went back upstairs to study for an exam. The girls began to clean up the kitchen and do the dishes. Waltz music drifted from the little brown radio on top of the sewing machine.

Cesare got his jacket from the back hall and slipped into it with a sigh. Days he worked as a laborer in the railroad, but now it was time for him to go to his night job as a watchman. The kitchen light shining on his face revealed the sudden weariness of it, the gray that was creeping into the mass of dark red hair, the lines etched around the black eyes that were more tired than fierce at this moment.

Silently Gianna loved him, remembering that deep in his heart burned a dream of his own that must be denied until other dreams were fulfilled. For his was the eternal dream of the immigrant—to go back to the old country once again, to embrace the aged parents he had not seen since he was seventeen.

Maria reached out and buttoned the top button of his jacket. She looked at him solicitously. "You all right, Cesare? You look tired. Maybe you should stay home tonight?"

He laughed heartily. "You crazy? Lose a night's pay so I can sit in a chair and listen to all your noise around this house?"

"Well, take it easy."

"Sure, sure, don't you worry. Cesare, he can take care of himself." He turned to his daughters. "Do your homework so you get all A's tomorrow. You all hear me? Good night."

He was gone, and the house seemed strangely quiet, echoing with the disturbing vitality he radiated. Maria poured herself another cup of coffee and sat down at the kitchen table.

Rose, seeing the look of worry, went to her, and kissed her forehead. "What's the matter, Mama? You're the one who looks tired."

Maria smiled a little and touched her daughter's comforting hand. "Yes, a little, I guess. I think about Papa and how hard he works to send everybody to school. Next year Paolo will be going to the seminary. The money he makes in the summer he will need for his expenses during the year. I think I will go back to the shop for awhile."

Gianna stared hard at her mother, sadness filling her heart at the immensity of her parents' struggle. "Life's awful hard sometimes, isn't it, Mama?"

Her mother's face softened. "Yes, life is hard. But you have to work for something, you have to have some goal. Otherwise your life is nothing. But one thing you must always remember."

"What, Mama?"

"As long as you have your family to love you, and

your religion to believe in, then you will always be all right. When you lose those two things then you are all alone in the world." Maria put down her coffee cup. "Finish the dishes and get on with the homework, all of you. Tomorrow is the first Friday of the month. You have to go to seven-thirty Mass."

A door opening and closing wakened Gianna. In the darkness she listened to the soft breathing of her sleeping sisters, then heard the murmured conversation downstairs. Her father had come home from his night shift and her mother had waited up for him, as always.

It was at this time of night, when their children were in bed, that they would discuss the bank loans and college tuitions and magically plan how to meet those payments.

And in the darkness Gianna vowed, I won't disappoint you, Mama and Papa. I'll try hard to make you proud of me.

2

In Columbus Park the trees had turned color and there was a crisp coolness in the air. The girls and boys hurried along the diagonal walks, shouting to each other, pushing, laughing. Only a few moments before they had marched from the parochial school to the corner in silent, somber precision, flanked by several stern-faced nuns. But now, the discipline of the day behind them, they were like freed animals. Here and there a fistfight erupted, and some of the boys, too long inactive, jumped the benches and climbed the trees and threw pebbles at the girls.

"Let's sit and talk a few minutes," Dominique said.

But Gianna shook her head. "Can't."

"Why not?"

"I have to go home and fry two eggplants and make sausage."

Dominique looked sympathetic. "How come you have to do it?"

"Because that's my job for today. Annamarie has to clean the house."

"Gee, I'm glad my mother doesn't have to work in a shop."

Gianna retorted defensively, "My mother doesn't

have to work in a shop either."

"My mother says your mother and father are foolish to work so hard. She says they should do like she does. She had my brothers quit school when they were sixteen and go to work. They bring their paychecks home every week and she gives them an allowance."

"Yes, but your brothers will always have to work in a shop. My mother and father want us to do something special."

"How come Paolo is going to be a priest?"

"Because he wants to give his life to God."

"Gee, it's hard to believe, him being a priest."

"Why?" Gianna demanded suspiciously.

"Because he's so nice looking."

"What's that got to do with it? Didn't you ever see a nice-looking young priest?"

Dominique giggled. "Nope. Did you?"

Gianna laughed then, too. "Me neither. Father Lorenzo's old as the hills, and the one before him was awfully old, too. But they start out young."

"Boy! Imagine having a nice priest like your brother! The women and girls would go to church all the time. Of course he might change his mind before he gets there."

"What do you mean by that?"

"Oh, you know. The girls like him. You can tell by the way they look at him."

"Well, he doesn't care about the girls."

"I wouldn't say that," Dominique said airily. "I see him talk to Laura Riccitelli sometimes."

"Big deal! If he's a priest he'll have to talk to all the girls, won't he?"

"That's true, now that you mention it. Only—"

"Only what?"

"It seems like he has a very special look in his eyes when he talks to her."

"Oh, you have a good imagination."

"Yes, I guess so. That's what my mother always says."

When Gianna opened the kitchen door she saw her grandmother rocking back and forth in the chair by the stove. How old Nonna looked, with her lined olive face and her snow-white braided hair, as if she had lived for all time and known all things.

Nonna glanced at the kitchen clock. "You're late," she said, but with a twinkle in her eyes. She smoothed the starched, flowered housedress over her fat knees. "You dream all the way home."

Gianna laughed. She put her books on the sewing machine. "I came right home. Only we talked a little on the way."

Nonna smiled wisely and pulled her shawl tighter around her shoulders. "You have to fry eggplant and make sausage. I put the eggplant to soak."

"I know, I know."

Nonna shook her head. "Such a girl," she murmured, almost to herself. "Just dream and talk and read books."

Upstairs Gianna found Annamarie already cleaning their bedroom. Her black hair was bound up in a kerchief and she was wearing an old dress that had a few buttons missing. She took time out from her mopping to give Gianna a hard stare. "How come you're so late? Did you go to the library?"

"Nope," was the muffled answer as Gianna pulled her white blouse over her head.

"Well, what took you so long? You have to fry two eggplants and make sausage."

"I know! Is there one more person in this house to tell me about it?"

"You needn't be so snippy."

"Well, you're awfully bossy today. When did Mama say you were going to boss me?"

"Somebody has to if we're ever going to get anything done around here."

"Gee, I wish Mama didn't have to work. I wish she could stay home like she used to," Gianna said.

"Well, it's this way now. So go do what you have to do."

Gianna went downstairs to the kitchen and took out the big cast-iron frying pan. Carefully, feeling her grandmother's sharp old eyes watching lest she waste a drop, she poured some oil into it from a large can.

"You put too much oil," the old woman commented critically, as she went on rocking.

Gianna turned the gas on low and went to the sink, where the sliced eggplant was being pressed in the colander with a heavy pan of water weighing it down. She squeezed the slices, one by one, letting the bitter brown juice drip into the sink. She put the eggplant into a clean dish and brought it to the stove. When her grandmother wasn't looking, she turned the gas a little higher so that the eggplant would cook faster.

There was a knock on the back door. Without an invitation, Zia Louisa walked in. She had been downtown and was dressed in her good black dress. The black made her sallow face more foreign looking, accentuated the drabness of her massive figure.

"You got the gas too high," she said. "You want to burn that poor eggplant?"

She dropped her bulky body into a chair at the table and let out a noisy sigh. Facing her mother, she asked, *"Come sta,* Mama? How's the world today?"

Which was never a good question to ask of Nonna, for it gave her a reason to contemplate just how bad things were.

She shrugged. *"Non ce male."*

This was her usual answer. Not bad, not good. It paved the way for the complaints. Today it was not her health that disturbed her. Today it was her husband. Every time she went out, he and his *comparo* went down to the wine barrel in the cellar. By the time she returned home she would find the two friends sitting beside the barrel singing old Italian folksongs, sometimes even dancing the tarantella.

"If I don't watch he is always at that barrel. Like a baby he is."

Louisa glowered at her mother over the cup of coffee Gianna poured for her. "This is some business," she muttered in Italian. "Some business that my sister has to go to work. She hasn't enough work right here at home? Cesare should have his head cut off. Some husband! Any day my husband would send *me* out to work! Better the children bring the money home to the parents. So who are these two that they put on airs that their children should go to college? Not only one, but all of them? Whoever heard of such nonsense?"

Nonna shrugged placidly.

"They take advantage of you, Mama. Making you come here. Why do they need you anyway? There are no small children."

"Cesare," Nonna murmured so that Gianna almost didn't hear. "Cesare, he wants a chaperone."

Louisa grunted and looked over at the eggplant. "See? It comes better when you don't put the gas too high. The other way you burn it, and who wants burnt eggplant?"

"Who wants eggplant anyway?"

Louisa grinned. "You don't like eggplant? What kind of Italian are you?"

"I don't mind eating it. But I hate to cook it."

"Some wife you'll make a man."

"Maybe I'll never get married."

Louisa looked over at her mother again. "You see what I mean? This one isn't even out of grade school yet and already she has crazy ideas. Well, I gotta go home now. Take care of yourself, Mama. See you tomorrow."

"Good-bye, Zia," Gianna said with a smile, trying to hide her grateful relief that her aunt was leaving.

"Good-bye, and don't turn up the gas under the eggplant the minute I go out the door, either."

When she had left, Nonna said, "You have to make sausage, too."

Gianna sighed. How she would have loved to curl up in a chair with a cup of coffee and a book. But that was a luxury she seldom got to indulge in any more.

When the eggplant had been fried a second time, in flour and egg, and layered in a casserole dish with tomato sauce and grated Parmesan cheese, Gianna set up the grinder and ground the sausage meat. She seasoned it with salt, pepper, and fennel seed; then rolled the casing over the end of a funnel and, with her thumb, deftly forced the pork meat through the casing.

Nonna smiled approvingly from the rocking chair. "You getting good," she commented. "You good enough to go into the sausage business yourself."

The back door opened and Maria came in. Gianna kissed her. "Gee, Mama, you look so tired. Hard day?"

Maria sank into a chair at the table after greeting her mother. "Every day's a hard day at that sweatshop. That boss, he's a slave driver."

"How about a cup of coffee, Mama?"

"Oh, that would really taste good right now."

As she drank the coffee, Maria looked at the newly made sausage rolled up on a plate. "It looks beautiful," she said. "You made it nice and lean. Did you put enough fennel seed? You know how Papa likes fennel seed."

"I put enough, Mama."

Nonna got up slowly and smoothed her housedress. "I go now," she said. "The old man will drink the wine barrel dry if I don't get home. He never had it so good as since I come here every day and don't see what he's doing. This year he will have to make twice as much wine."

"Well, we'll see you tomorrow," Maria said, going to the door with her mother.

Nonna lived two houses away, in a six-family tenement she owned. Despite the many years she had been in America, her life was still enclosed and bordered by this Italian Catholic neighborhood. She spoke her native language most of the time and followed the old ways and the old customs; there had never been any desire to change. In this world all was familiar to her. This was the way she had lived and this was the way she would die.

"Nonna's getting old," Maria sighed. "I don't think she's as well as she used to be. Gianna, did you get the vinegar peppers up from the cellar?"

"Yes, Mama."

"Good. Now go get the paper before your father comes home."

3

Gianna woke to hear her father's lusty rendition of "Figaro" from the bathroom, and she smiled drowsily. She knew how much Sunday meant to Cesare, how he looked forward to it. All week he worked the seven-to-four shift in the railroad and the six-to-twelve nighttime shift at the warehouse. Sunday was his day off from both jobs and he enjoyed every minute of it.

When the weather was good he worked in the backyard, pruning fruit trees, planting seeds, weeding, raking. Or if the weather was bad he would do repairs in the house, catching up on small jobs. In the afternoon he would go to Waterside Park with Leonardo, his *comparo,* and play *bocci,* or else they would go to the club and have a game of pinochle over a bottle of wine.

And now Cesare swept through the hall calling out, "Time for church!"

Time for the rest of the family to go to church, but not him. Like most of the other men in the neighborhood he went to church only for baptisms, weddings, and funerals. After all, when God saw that a man had such a religious wife and such devout children, one of them even going to be a priest, God had to know that this was a good man. How could a bad man produce such a religious family?

Occasionally, perhaps after a scathing sermon from Father Lorenzo on the subject of all the delinquent fathers and husbands who were headed for hell, the family would worry about Cesare's chances of ever getting into heaven. They would argue with him until he finally lost his temper, and then they would leave him alone and trust to God's kindness to overlook his religious slackness.

"Well, he is a good man," Maria would say then. "I guess God understands him." She was likely to add, a little caustically, "Even if nobody else does."

The air was cold as a wind swept through the bedroom, but from downstairs came the warm spicy smell of *braciole* browning in hot oil. Maria had already started the Sunday dinner.

Gianna rolled over in bed and watched Rose as she stood at the bureau combing her hair. She wondered if she would ever be as pretty as her sister. Maybe when she started to wear make-up and when her body began to fill out. Right now her skin was sallow and her body straight and skinny.

Rose had thick, wavy dark hair and soft, pretty features. Today she looked aglow with happiness. Her brown eyes were shining. She turned from the mirror and faced her sisters. "I have something to tell you," she said.

They were suddenly wide awake, sitting up in their double bed with their arms hugging their knees.

"I have a date this afternoon."

"A date?"

"Who with? You never mentioned anyone."

"Mario Gennetti. I met him at school, he's in some of my classes. He's graduating when I do. He's going to be a teacher, too."

The questions tumbled from their lips. Was he good looking? Did she love him? Did he love her? Was she going to marry him?

She laughed, but the answers were already there in the dark glow of her eyes, the flush of her cheeks. "Look, it's our first date so don't get me married yet. I didn't tell Mama and Papa. I have to tell Mama first and ask her to tell Papa not to treat him like a son-in-law. You know how he is. He'll ask him a hundred questions. Where did his family come from? How much money is he going to make? I don't want to be embarrassed, and I don't want him scared off."

She picked up her missal from the bureau. "Well, see you downstairs."

When she had left the room Gianna and Annamarie stared at each other. "She's in love," Gianna said. She looked over at Rose's bed, already neatly made up. "Maybe one of these days we'll each get to have a bed. Sooner than we think, maybe."

Annamarie laughed. "It's only her first date. You're worse than Papa."

The kitchen was a bright warm place on a cold morning. There was a coal fire in the old black stove, and Maria was frying meatballs. The *braciole,* tied-up beef rolls stuffed with parsley, garlic, and cheese, now simmered in tomato sauce on a back burner.

Turning from the stove, Maria said to Cesare, "Why do you always spend so much time reading the Classifieds? You're not looking for a job, and you can't afford to buy anything."

"Because they say something about the times."

She still did not understand. "What can they say? Someone wants to sell a house, someone wants a job."

Cesare smiled at his daughters. "You see? Women, they don't understand these things. These ads, they tell you how the country's going. Whether things get better or worse."

"Well, whatever. They won't change your life one way or the other, whether they have more ads or less. If you want to think about something, I think we should buy a cemetery lot. They're opening up a new section in St. Lawrence's."

Cesare gaped at her, his black eyes narrowing. "What's a matter? I look like I'm getting ready to die?"

"You don't have to die before you start to think where you're going to be buried."

Cesare laughed and beat his chest. "Hear that? A-1 like always! When I'm not A-1 then maybe I stop and think about cemetery lots."

Maria looked anxious. "But the Catholic cemeteries may be full by that time."

"So bury me in a Jewish one. I won't know the difference."

They all looked at him in horror. "Papa!"

"Why? You think they don't dig as good graves in a Jewish cemetery as a Catholic? They always look buried to me. And one more thing—one last request—when you bury me make it near the fence, so everybody he goes by, he says, 'There's Cesare Dellesanto, that A-1 boy! Look how good the flowers grow on his grave.' "

There was a knock on the door, and it was Leonardo, Cesare's *comparo,* who always came on Sunday mornings.

Gianna loved to listen to the conversations between the two men, for often they spoke of the old country, which she had never seen. And her father would recall the home he had left, the low dark roof glimmering in the warm Italian sun, the olive trees green and golden. She especially liked the stories the two men told. In the years of her growing up she had spent many a cold winter's afternoon in a corner of the kitchen, close to the heat of the stove, listening to the strange tales.

Leonardo had one particular horror story about the man in his village who was suspected of being a werewolf. One Saturday night when the men had been out drinking, the man disappeared suddenly from the group, and a moment later there was the howling cry and the shadow of a wolf in their path. The men had sobered up quite quickly after that and run home as fast as their feet could take them.

And then there were the stories of the Black Hand, told almost in whispers, of men who died mysterious deaths, suddenly, and without the killers ever being found.

It was time to leave for Mass. Maria said to Cesare, "Watch the sauce. Give it a stir once in awhile. Make sure it doesn't burn."

Cesare waved his hand. "You no worry about the sauce. I take good care."

"And don't add nothing to it," was her final warning. "It's already seasoned."

In church Dominique leaned over the next pew and whispered to Gianna, "Meet me outside after. I have something to tell you."

Dominique's mother, dark and saturnine, dressed in black from head to toe, gave her daughter a sharp nudge in the ribs. Dominique and Gianna both returned to their rosaries.

"So what's the big exciting news?" Gianna wanted to know when she saw Dominique after Mass.

"We got a new girl in our house."

Gianna was disappointed. "So what's so great about that?"

"Because she's different, that's what."

"Different? How's she different?"

"She's Protestant, and her mother's divorced. And her mother's got bleached blonde hair!"

"Well, that's different. What's her name?"

"Muriel. Muriel Martin. And that's not all."

"What? What? What else?"

"Her mother has a boyfriend."

"Boyfriend! Her *mother?*"

"Only she doesn't look like a mother, if you know what I mean. I mean, she's not fat, she's very thin, and she wears kind of tight clothes. In fact, she even wears slacks a lot. But Muriel's very interesting. She's been a lot of places and done a lot of things. We could go see her this afternoon if you want."

"I don't know about today. It all depends. My sister Rose has a boyfriend coming over. I have to see him."

"Rose?"

"Shh. My mother doesn't know yet."

The first thing Maria did when she entered her kitchen was to taste the sauce. She looked suspiciously at Cesare, who had come in from the yard. "You did add something," she accused him. "I don't know what, but you put something."

"Let me taste it, Mama," Rose said, taking the big wooden spoon from her mother. She considered, then looked straight at her father, a twinkle in her eyes, and said, "It's fennel seed. That's what you put in."

"What did you do that for?" Maria demanded. "I told you it was already seasoned."

"Oh, women!" Cesare shouted. "What you know about cooking, eh? Why you think chefs are always men? You ever see a woman chef? It's because men, they have the taste, they have the knack."

"You have the knack all right. A knack for butting in where you're supposed to stay out."

"So crucify me," he said benevolently, as he left the room and headed for the yard again.

"So far we've been lucky," Maria said. "But just

imagine some day when he's had a few glasses and reaches for the cloves instead."

Rose said, "Mama, I have something to tell you. I have a date this afternoon."

"A date?" Maria was all alertness now. "Who's the man? You never said nothing about a man."

Rose looked dreamy again. "I met him at school. He's going to be a teacher, too. He's graduating when I do."

"And what's his name?"

"Mario Gennetti."

Gianna saw the tension in her mother's face relax then. It was all right. He was one of them.

"You'll meet him this afternoon. Only"—her face clouded a little—"do you suppose you could have a talk with Papa? I mean—this is my first date with Mario. I don't want Papa to ask him a million questions and treat him like a son-in-law. I mean, this isn't like when you were young."

Maria hugged her. "Don't you worry. I'll have a talk with him."

"Where is Papa?" Gianna asked.

"He went back outside. Tell him we'll be eating soon. I'll call you when I throw the macaroni."

Gianna found her father sitting in the grape arbor, smoking his cigar and enjoying the autumn sunshine.

"Mama says she'll call us when she throws the macaroni."

"Good."

The grape vines were low now; Cesare always cut

them down in the fall. In the garden area the plant stalks and leaves had been pulled up and the earth smoothed over.

"Papa?"

"Yeah?"

She sat beside him in the open grape arbor and felt the sun warm and golden on her face. The smoke from her father's cigar was strong and heady.

"What's the big problem today?" he asked.

"Papa, what's the real difference between Catholics and Protestants?"

"Why? What's a difference to you?"

"I was just wondering."

He waved his hands as if to dismiss the whole subject. "It's nothing for you to worry about. You're Catholic."

"I just want to know, what's the real difference? Is it just like in politics where there are Democrats and Republicans?"

He thought for a moment, puffing on his cigar. "Well, maybe you could say that. Same difference maybe. Always there's two sides to a fence. Same thing in religion, same thing in politics. Two sides. One side's right and one side's wrong."

"How do you know which side is right?"

His black brows knit together in dark impatience. "Whichever side you're on, that's the right side."

"But how do you know, Papa?"

"What you mean? How I know? If I'm on Catholic side, then that's the right side. Take my word for it."

"But Protestants believe in God, don't they?"

He shrugged. "I suppose so."

"Then don't they think they're on the right side, too?"

"Sure! Everybody, he thinks he's on the right side. That's why everybody in this world fights and gets into wars. That's what makes the world go like merry-go-round. Why you bother me with problems of the world on an empty stomach, eh? I don't have nothing of my own to worry about? Look, you don't go worrying about Protestants. You're Catholic and you'll be Catholic all your life. You'll marry one and your children will be Catholic. So why you have a hundred questions about something you don't need to know about?"

"I just like to know things, Papa."

Sunday dinner was always especially pleasant. Today there was baked ziti with the *braciole* and meatballs, and apples for dessert.

As they lingered over the coffee, Maria said, "Cesare, Rose has a date this afternoon."

"A date?" Cesare stared at his oldest daughter. "Who you have a date with?"

Rose looked a little nervous. "His name is Mario Gennetti, Papa."

Her father relaxed, as her mother had, and smiled. "So, how you meet him?"

"At school. He's going to be a teacher, too."

Maria said, "Cesare, when he comes, treat him just like everybody else."

"What you mean—like everybody else? He's different?"

"You know what I mean. This is their first date. Don't act like he's a future son-in-law."

"What you think—I'm a dope? I don't know how to act?"

"You know what I mean. Don't ask him where his family came from, or a hundred questions about himself. Just be friendly and polite."

Cesare seemed miffed. "You think I don't know how to act? I have almost a whole family going to college and you think I don't know how to act when my daughter, she brings home a boyfriend?"

He looked back at Rosa. "You like him, this—this Mario—what's his name—Gennetti?"

She smiled. "Yes, Papa. I think he likes me a lot, too."

"So what's the problem?"

The talk turned to the coming wedding of Zia Louisa's son, Philip. He had the distinction of being the only one in the whole family who had ever been divorced. However, there was no scandal attached to his divorce because he had been married by a justice of the peace the first time and his marriage had never been recognized by the church. So now he was marrying again. This time he would have a big church wedding.

"You know," Gianna reflected, "if a person wanted to have a dozen wives or husbands he could just keep getting married by a justice of the peace, and then when he wanted to stay married he could get married by the church and be in good standing for the rest of his life."

Her mother and sisters gaped at her in disbelief, and Paolo and Cesare smiled. "Gianna!" her mother said. "Where do you get these ideas? This is what you learn from all those books you read?"

Gianna shrugged. "Well, that's what it amounts to, anyway. Because if somebody got married in the church to begin with and then got divorced and wanted to get married again, he would live in sin for the rest of his life and the church wouldn't even bury him."

"Who are you all of a sudden? All of a sudden you're God's own critic?"

"I didn't criticize God."

"It's the same thing. When you criticize the church, you criticize God. You better say some prayers in a hurry before God turns his head on you, you shameful girl. Oh, that I should hear a daughter of mine say such things. Mother of God, forgive this girl."

Paolo said, rising from the table, "Mama, don't worry about it. I have the feeling God, too, can understand the questions."

And Cesare laughed loudly. "Such a daughter I got! How that little head holds so many worries of the world I don't know. What's a matter, Gianna mia? You got nothing in your own life you can worry about?"

"I still don't think it's right."

They waited in the living room for Mario Gennetti, and when he rang the bell Rose almost jumped. She looked around at her parents and sisters. "Now remember, treat him just like a date. No questions."

She opened the front door, and when she returned she had with her a tall, good-looking young man with black wavy hair and hazel eyes.

"This is Mario Gennetti, Mama and Papa."

It was difficult to think of Mario as a casual date when he looked at Rose with such affection, but the family followed her orders and no one asked a single question.

When they were leaving, Cesare shook hands with him and said, "You come again. Soon." It was his way of saying, "You're accepted, you're welcome in this house."

Mario smiled down at Rose. "You can be sure of that, Mr. Dellesanto."

After they left, Cesare smiled. "I think—I think we hear wedding bells not too far off. You see the way he looks at her? Like a queen."

"She is a queen," Maria said. "She's your daughter, isn't she?"

"This is their first date," Gianna said laughingly. "How can you hear wedding bells already?"

Her father's black eyes flashed. "You know these things when you have children."

"You mean a little voice tells you?" she teased him.

"Never mind the wisecracks. A father knows what's good for his children."

4

It wasn't until the following Sunday afternoon that Gianna finally met Muriel Martin.

"Where are you going?" Maria had asked as Gianna put on her sweater.

"Over to Dominique's for awhile."

"Well, be on time for supper."

"I will."

Dominique lived on the third floor of a six-family tenement across the street. As Gianna passed the second-floor landing people were coming out of a flat where a wake was being held. She caught a glimpse of a casket and dull red candlelight, and the waxen face of a young man. John Piscitelli. She remembered him now. He had been sick with tuberculosis for a long time.

The smells of food lingered in the hall. Veal and peppers, sausage, *suffrito,* pastry, fresh coffee. One thing was sure. The mourners would eat well.

She hurried to the third floor. Dominique opened the door as soon as Gianna knocked on it. "Come on in, but be quiet. My mother's taking a nap."

Gianna sat down at the kitchen table. "I just saw the wake."

"Ooh, don't mention it. I can't sleep at night. I'll be so glad when that poor guy is finally buried. All I think of in the dark is him lying down there in the coffin. Every time I pass the door I can see him. . . . Well, you want to go visit Muriel?"

Gianna shrugged, feigning indifference, hiding her curiosity. "I don't care. What else is there to do?"

"Well, I told her I'd probably bring you over today. She's dying to meet you. You'll like her, Gianna. She's awfully nice. Her mother, too. They're very friendly people."

"How come they're living here if they're so different?"

"It's only for a short while, until her mother gets married again."

"Her mother's getting married again?"

"Yeah. Her boyfriend is nice. Maybe you'll get to meet him, too."

This certainly was going to be an interesting afternoon, Gianna thought. "Well, let's go now then, all right? Because I have to be on time for supper. You know how my parents are about being home on time."

"Sure. Come on."

Gianna was surprised when Dominique went to Muriel's living-room door instead of the kitchen. People in the neighborhood always went to the kitchen, even best company. The kitchen was where hospitality began.

"Muriel's mother likes people to go to the front door," Dominique explained. "Especially now. Their kitchen is still messy from moving and all."

She knocked at the door and a girl opened it. "Hi, Muriel, this is Gianna."

Muriel Martin struck a chord of jealousy in Gianna in that first meeting. She was so pretty, with her golden hair in a long, smooth pageboy and her large, violet-blue eyes rimmed in long black lashes.

She smiled warmly at Gianna. "Oh, I'm so glad to meet you. I've been hearing about you all week."

The jealousy waned. "You have?"

"Oh, yes. Dominique's always talking about you and your family, how great you are. Come on in. I'm so glad you came. It's such a dull, dreary day."

The Martins had a railroad flat like everyone else in the building. But Gianna was sure no one else had a flat decorated like this one. She especially envied Muriel her room. There was a lovely walnut bedroom set with flowered draperies and a bedspread to match. And a kidney-shaped dressing table with a flounced skirt that matched the draperies and bedspread, the top glittering with cologne bottles and a silver dresser set.

However, Gianna's envy vanished when she saw the kitchen. She had never seen a sloppier one in her whole life. There seemed to be dirty dishes everywhere, on the porcelain-topped table, in the sink, on the drainboard, even on the stove. She was used to her mother's kitchen, where the dishes were washed after every meal, the floor waxed until it shone, and the stove polished like black gold.

In the midst of all the chaos Muriel's mother was putting up white polka-dot curtains. She was pretty, and thin in her black slacks and coral sweater.

Mrs. Martin smiled warmly when Dominique introduced Gianna. "Well, so you're Gianna. We've heard lots about you. I'm so glad Muriel will have such nice friends. I was a little afraid at first—"

Muriel said warningly, "Mother—"

"Well, I'll tell you what, girls. You have to excuse this kitchen. What with moving and all we're not quite settled. I've been so busy with other things—you understand. But if you girls will go in the living room I'll bring you some tea and cake. Would you like that?"

They grinned happily, not used to being served in the living room.

"All right then. Muriel, why don't you show the girls the albums? Maybe they'd like to see the trips you've been on."

"Okay, Mother. Come on, girls."

Muriel led the way through the bedrooms to the living room. The Martins' kitchen might be a mess at this moment but their living room was very nice, Gianna thought, now that she had more time to look at it.

It was the same size and shape as Dominique's. But instead of straight ecru panels at the windows there were bright green-and-white flowered draperies, and white window shades instead of the usual dark green. While everyone else in the neighborhood had linoleum in the living room, the Martins had a pale green carpet.

Even the mantelpiece looked different. It was painted white, with a mirror over it. On the shelf was an assortment of bisque figurines, and a copper bowl of philodendron.

The furniture was pretty, too. Plushy, with white crocheted chair-back sets on the maroon sofa and dark green chairs.

As Muriel went to get the albums, Dominique whispered to Gianna, "Didn't I tell you they were different? I wish our living room looked like this. And Muriel says they'll use it all winter, too, not shut it off like we do."

Muriel returned, smiling, a big album in her arms. She sat between the two girls on the couch, and from then on they were a part of her world, a world they had scarcely imagined before. In her short lifetime she had been more places, done more things, than anybody they had ever known. Except, of course, Dominique's uncle who was a sailor.

In some of the earlier pictures there was a man with his arm around her mother. "That's my father," Muriel said a little wistfully. "He and my mother are divorced."

"Do you ever see him?"

"Oh, yes! Every week. On Saturdays usually. He comes and picks me up and we go away for the day, just the two of us."

"Where do you go?"

Muriel's eyes shone. "Oh, all kinds of places. Sometimes we go to New York to the Zoo and the Planetarium, and sometimes the Radio City Music Hall to see the stage show."

"Oh, tell us about Radio City!"

So Muriel described the organ rising up out of the floor, and the line of Rockettes kicking up their legs in beautiful precision.

"And then we have dinner at Toffenetti's," she finished off grandly.

"What's Toffenetti's?"

"One of the big restaurants in New York. I always order the same thing. Baked Virginia ham and candied sweet potatoes."

"Gee, you sure have a wonderful time out of life," Gianna remarked awefully.

Muriel's face was suddenly wistful, shadowed. She looked down and fingered her skirt for a moment. "Yes, I guess you could say that."

Mrs. Martin came in then with a silver tea service, and some china cups and saucers. On the tray were also paper napkins, monogrammed, and silver forks and spoons.

"You fix your tea," she said. "I'll put it on the coffee table here. I'll get the cake."

She returned with a large store-bought chocolate layer cake and some china plates. "Help yourselves, girls."

She sat down near the window and lit a cigarette. Gianna and Dominique stared at her in undisguised shock, and Muriel looked a little embarrassed.

Seeing their expressions, Mrs. Martin laughed gaily. "Don't look so shocked, girls. Haven't you ever seen a woman smoke?"

Dumbly they shook their heads.

"Well, this is a sheltered neighborhood," she said. "But don't look so shocked. Women smoke everywhere these days."

But not in our world, Gianna thought.

The Martins had a piano, so after the tea and cake Muriel played the latest popular songs and Gianna and Dominique watched and hummed along. Mrs. Martin went to get dressed for her boyfriend who was coming later to take her and Muriel to dinner and a movie. When she returned to the living room she was wearing a chic black dress and a double string of pearls at the throat. And there was a fragrance of perfume, delicate, exquisite.

Dominique said shyly, "Gee, Mrs. Martin, you sure look nice."

Gianna, too, was impressed. Mrs. Martin looked like a glamorous movie star. It was strange to think of her as a mother, she looked so young.

Her boyfriend came about four o'clock, a nice-looking man with gray hair and a pleasant smile. It was obvious he was very much in love with Mrs. Martin. He also seemed quite fond of Muriel for he kissed her when he came in.

It was with regret that Gianna said she must go

home for supper. She had had such a lovely afternoon. She had seen and heard enough to think about for quite some time to come. And she was sorry now that Muriel wouldn't be going to parochial school with her and Dominique.

As she and Dominique were leaving, Mrs. Martin said, "I want you girls to come as often as you like. You're always welcome."

Out in the hall Dominique asked excitedly, "Well, didn't you like them? Aren't they interesting?"

"They sure are," Gianna agreed. "I hated to leave."

"Wouldn't you like to have the clothes she wears? And the good times she has? Always going places and seeing different things? I wouldn't mind changing places with her."

"Yeah, me too. She sure is lucky. Listen, I'd better get that book you borrowed from me."

It was raining when Gianna left Dominique's flat, and Muriel and Mrs. Martin were getting into the boyfriend's car. Their laughter rang out in the rainy afternoon. Gianna waved to them as the car pulled away from the curb. She thought of the dinner and movie they would be going to, and how nice that would be. She had never gone out to dinner in her life, and as for movies—well, they were few and far between.

Movies were like Italian pastry, they were luxuries in life.

The cooking smells of the neighborhood seeped out

of the homes into the rain. Even in bad times the air at suppertime was spicy and fragrant. Garlic and anchovies browning in olive oil, bitter broccoli steaming, homemade sausage sweetly aromatic, tomato sauce that had been simmering on the back of a stove for hours and hours. And *pasta e fava* and *pasta fagioli.* Oregano and parsley and basil, and chicken in vinegar.

Chicken. Nothing was wasted. The claws were put in sauce, even the heads were eaten, and the chicken fat rendered for other cooking.

Beans. All kinds. Cabbage and beans, macaroni and beans, rice and beans.

Macaroni. There was nothing Maria wouldn't cook with macaroni. Cauliflower and salt pork, potatoes, beans, meat, shellfish, chicken.

Yes, no matter how bad times were, there was always something good cooking.

Gianna wondered what Muriel would order for supper. But when she opened the back door and smelled *pizzaiole,* chuck steak braised with tomatoes and cheese, she no longer envied Muriel Martin.

"Where've you been?" Maria asked. "You look like a drowned cat."

Gianna shook her hair free from the kerchief and held her hands over the stove. "I went to see Dominique. I told you."

"Well, go change your clothes before you catch pneumonia."

A short while later Annamarie came into the bedroom looking for Gianna for supper. "What's gotten into you, Gianna?"

"Why?"

"I don't know. You look—different."

Gianna couldn't hold it in any longer. She had to tell someone. "Close the door."

"Oh," groaned Annamarie, "you don't have a boyfriend, too!"

Gianna grimaced. "Funny, funny." Annamarie closed the door. "I had the most wonderful afternoon!"

"At Dominique's?"

"No, silly. I have a new friend. She just moved in across the hall from Dominique. Her name is Muriel Martin."

She told Annamarie all about the afternoon, and her sister, too, was impressed although not overwhelmed.

"I wouldn't go out of my way to mention Muriel and her mother to Mama and Papa," Annamarie cautioned.

"No, I don't figure to. I didn't lie though. I did go to Dominique's."

"I don't think Mama and Papa would like the idea that Mrs. Martin is divorced and has a boyfriend. They aren't used to women doing these things."

"She smokes, too!"

"How can you say she's so nice?"

"But she is! She's one of the nicest people I ever met. She made us feel like—like queens."

"Well, I still say, keep it to yourself as long as you can."

The Martins became an exciting part of Gianna's and Dominique's lives. Sunday afternoons were something to look forward to now. In the Martins' flat there was always a pleasant, interesting time to be had. Muriel had a game called Monopoly and sometimes they played this for hours. And of course there was always a tea party. But the best thing of all was when Muriel described her day with her father.

From her living-room windows Gianna had a good view of the tenement in which Muriel lived, and she began to watch for Muriel's father on Saturdays. She would see him drive up in his shiny black car and Muriel would run out to meet him, dressed in her very best clothes. Her father would kiss her when she got into the car, and then they would drive off for their day of pleasure, while Gianna would return to dull household chores.

Once Maria asked, "What are you watching, Gianna?"

"Muriel going with her father."

By now Maria and Cesare knew about the Martins. "So? You think that's so wonderful?" Maria asked.

"She has such exciting times."

"Well, I think it's much more wonderful to have a father who lives with you every day than one who just makes a big deal out of taking you for a good time once a week. What about her mother? Don't you think she'd rather have a husband who lives with her?"

"I don't think so."

"Why not? He looked like a nice man from here."

"She has a boyfriend. They're going to get married."

"So that's the kind of people you associate with? If your father knew—"

"He knows."

"He knows!"

"Sure. In fact, I introduced him to Mrs. Martin on the street once. He thought she was a nice woman."

"I suppose she's good looking?"

"Yes, she's very pretty and very young. She doesn't even look like a mother. Haven't you seen her?"

"Not that I know of." Maria's attitude indicated that she had no inclination to see or hear about Mrs. Martin.

"Oh, Mama, what have you got against her?"

Maria drew herself up stiffly. "I'm not God. It's not for me to judge other people. I suppose if she wants to get divorced and get another husband it's her business, her conscience, not mine. But why do you think she's so wonderful? I just don't understand it."

Gianna didn't answer. Her mother would never understand if she told her. How could you describe the atmosphere in the Martins' home? Where mealtime was any time you were hungry, and food was quickly and effortlessly prepared? No sausage to make, no eggplant to fry, nothing to cook that took hours and hours. A dinner was most likely to be steak and boiled potatoes and canned peas and store-bought pie or cake. And everything served on pretty dishes and a tablecloth on the kitchen table. Mrs. Martin's kitchen had improved, Gianna was happy to reflect. She hadn't seen any dirty dishes lately, and the floor even looked waxed these days.

Life at the Martins' was pleasant and casual. They could eat meat on Friday and if they missed church on Sunday they didn't have to go to confession because there was no confession in their church.

Yes, it would be difficult to explain to her mother.

5

Christmas Eve, and in the light snowfall the neighborhood became suddenly, magically, beautiful. Gianna had gone to the store for a last-minute quart of milk, and now, walking home, she slowed her steps, as if in so doing she could longer savor all the happiness that sang inside her.

The tenements glowed like illuminated bricks in the white darkness. Where shades were not pulled down she saw families moving about in lighted rooms. In some flats the trees were already decorated and the colored bulbs glimmered softly on shining ornaments and glittering tinsel. And she saw people laughing and touching and wrapping gifts and cooking the Christmas Eve seafood dinner. Later tonight the streets would be alive with people hurrying to Midnight Mass, and the cold air would echo their happy voices.

Gianna had come to her own house now. It stood out from the tenements like a small jewel. The tree wouldn't be decorated until after supper, but the house was full of lights. She saw her father and brothers in the living room, and caught a glimpse of her mother and sisters in the kitchen.

She smiled a little, remembering the weeks that had

been spent in preparing for Christmas. Every floor had been scrubbed and waxed, every piece of furniture lovingly polished with lemon oil. Curtains had been taken down and starched and stretched, bedspreads washed, crocheted doilies blocked.

For days the house had smelled of the Christmas cooking and baking.

Tonight was a very special Christmas Eve, for Rose and Mario had become engaged that afternoon. They had announced their plans to be married after their graduation.

Rose wanted a small, quiet wedding, but Cesare was indignant.

"What you mean—a small, quiet wedding?" he demanded. "Who the hell ever heard of a small, quiet Italian wedding?"

It was almost sacrilege. No matter how poor the family, there was always a dinner and a band and a big reception.

Rose felt guilty about getting married so soon after graduating. "I'll help you out anyway," she said. "I'll give you something out of my pay every week."

But Cesare said, "When you get married, it's between you and your husband. We'll get along."

As Gianna opened the front gate a familiar voice called out her name in the darkness. She turned and saw Eddy hurrying down the street, carrying a bag of Christmas gifts and a small suitcase.

With the street light shining down on him he looked very big and handsome, and she loved him dearly. She loved her other brothers, too, but Julio was older and more reserved and Paolo inclined to be introspective and moody at times. Eddy was the one to whom she could confide her most secret dreams, Eddy was the brother with whom she could laugh the most. He was more than a brother; he was her best friend, her closest confidante.

He had reached the gate. His dark eyes were shining, and the snow glistened wetly on his black, curly hair. He leaned over his bag of gifts and kissed her. "Merry Christmas, little sister."

"Merry Christmas to you, too, big brother."

"What are they doing, making you go to the store on a holiday eve?"

She laughed. "You know how it is in our house. We're always running out of something. Why are you so late? Julio got here this morning. He said you had to work but you'd be here by late afternoon."

"Well, I waited for a ride. There's no point wasting money on a train if I can get a free car ride."

As Gianna walked with her brother around the back of the house, she was bubbling over with all the things she had to tell him.

"Rose got engaged this afternoon, she's getting married in June. Oh, and thanks for the book you sent me on that excavation in Crete. It really helped me with that paper I had to write. The teacher was quite impressed with my knowledge."

The backyard was splendidly white and silent, the leafless branches of the fruit trees casting long shadows on the snow, the dress factory a blob of blackness in the night.

Gianna opened the kitchen door and the heat of the stove blasted out at her. Her mother was watching the sizzling smelts browning goldenly in the large black frying pan. Tomato sauce with lobster simmered on the back of the stove, and there was a big dish of shrimp already fried.

Over on top of the sewing machine, for lack of a better place, were the pastries: the huge round loaf of *panettone.* filled with raisins and candied fruit, and the silver tray of *zeppole,* the fried dough dipped in honey and dusted with confectioners sugar.

Annamarie was setting the kitchen table with the best dishes on a flowered tablecloth, and Rose was at the sink washing the dishes and pans that had already accumulated.

"Eddy's home!" Gianna announced.

Her mother's face brightened, and she turned from her cooking to throw her arms around her son and kiss him noisily. "I thought you wouldn't get here in time for supper!" Then she pushed him away laughingly. "I'll burn the smelts!"

Gianna put the milk in the icebox. "Mama's happy now that she has all her boys home," she said teasingly.

"I'm happy when I got all my children home, never mind just the boys." Maria was always insistent that she loved all her children the same, that no one had a higher place in her favor than the others.

"Oh, Mama, you don't have to explain. I know. And

next year you'll have three to come home."

Gianna looked across the room at Paolo, who was hanging a red crepe-paper bell over a light. "And next year you'll be coming home from college, too."

He smiled back at her, then turned away. But she had seen the look on his face, in his eyes, and she remembered what Dominique had said. Since that day she had watched him more carefully. Once she had seen him walking through Columbus Park with Laura Riccitelli, and they were laughing over something. She never mentioned it to anyone, least of all her mother.

Maria was saying, "Yes, Paolo, not too long from now you'll be on your way to being a priest."

He seemed not to hear her. He doesn't want to go after all, Gianna thought, and he's afraid to say it.

But that was nonsense. Of course he wanted to go. Paolo had always wanted to be a priest, ever since he was a small boy, getting up in the cold mornings before the rest of them to hurry over to the church to serve as altar boy. There had never been the slightest doubt that he would be a priest.

Julio came into the kitchen then, and he and Eddy pulled Maria away from the stove and under the mistletoe in the doorway. They kissed and hugged her until she protested breathlessly.

"The smelts!" she cried out laughingly. "Someone turn the smelts!"

Cesare came to the doorway, his face flushed from wine. "See how she's glad to have you home? You know how she worries about you? Me, she don't care nothing about. Me, she don't worry about what I eat or how I sleep. But always she's worrying, 'I wonder how my Julio is, I wonder how my Eddy is. I wonder what did they have for supper last night, I wonder what did they have for supper tonight, I wonder what will they have for supper tomorrow night.' "

Julio laughed. "Believe me, Mama, we don't get anything like your cooking."

Maria's face clouded and she glared at Cesare. "You see? I told you they don't get good cooking at those fancy colleges."

"I didn't say that, Mama. I just said it wasn't like yours."

"What's that supposed to mean?"

"It's different."

She nodded understandingly. "I know. American food. Quick, quick, quick. Well, never mind. Some day you marry a nice Italian girl and you can eat right again."

Eddy laughed then. Maria looked at him suspiciously. "What's so funny?"

"He's got a girl, Mama. And she's not Italian."

Maria turned on Julio, her eyes worried, and everyone in the room stared.

Julio said proudly, "Yes, I've got a girl, Mama."

"What you mean, you got a girl?" his father demanded.

"Look, why is everyone getting so excited? Because I have a girl? I'm not going to be a priest. Why shouldn't I have a girl?"

"What's she like, Julio?" Rose asked, and the other two sisters crowded in on him, full of questions. What did she look like, what color hair did she have?

When he said she had blonde hair and blue eyes, Cesare asked, "What's her name, this girl?"

"Valerie. Valerie Courtney."

"What kind of name is that?"

"It's a beautiful name, Papa. And she's a beautiful girl. Isn't she, Eddy?"

He turned to his brother, who looked sorry now that he had brought up the subject. What had started out as a ribbing had turned almost into a family crisis. "Yes, she's beautiful, all right. And rich, too."

Julio glowered at him. "Now why'd you have to say that?"

Cesare shrugged. "Well, that's nice. You got a beautiful rich girl. But she's not Italian, no?"

"Afraid not, Papa. Her people are originally from England."

"So she's only a girlfriend, right?"

"Right, Papa, she's only a girlfriend."

"But you remember something. You got a long way to go before you're a doctor, so you watch it, you know what I mean?"

Julio laughed then and squeezed his father's shoulder. "Papa, stop worrying about it. Mama, throw the macaroni, we're all starved."

After dinner, while the men worked on the tree lights in the living room, the kitchen became again a woman's place, as it always was when there was work to be done. Annamarie handed the dishpan to Rose. "Mama's happy because she's got her boys back."

"And now she's got an extra one," Rose said in a dreamy voice.

Her mother hugged her. "That's right. Now I got a future son-in-law."

"And maybe a future daughter-in-law, too," Gianna said mischievously.

"Never mind a future daughter-in-law!" Maria snapped.

A roar of laughter came from the living room. "They're telling jokes," Gianna said, trying to hear.

Her mother handed her a dish towel. "Well, you don't listen to men's jokes."

"Why?"

"Because men tell dirty jokes, they're not for innocent young girls to hear."

"What kind of dirty jokes do men tell, Mama?"

"Will you stop worrying about their dirty jokes? Your business right now is to dry the dishes."

"I can't dry them till Rose washes them."

"Here, smarty-pants," Rose said, rinsing a stack of dishes and placing them in the drainer.

"Well, some day I have to hear these jokes. They must be awfully funny the way they're laughing in there."

"You wouldn't understand them anyway," Rose said.

"Why?"

"They're about things you know nothing about."

Maria looked closely at her oldest daughter. "And you know so much about all those things?"

Rose laughed. "Mama, I'm engaged to be married, and almost ready to be graduated from college. I sure hope I know something about life. Don't you trust me?"

"I trust you. It's the men in this world I don't trust."

"Don't let Mario hear you say that. He wouldn't feel flattered."

"Mario's different. I trust him. You made a good choice."

The girls all laughed so hard then that the men looked in from the living room. "What's so funny in here?" Julio asked.

"Oh, go back to your dirty jokes," Gianna said.

He looked at her in puzzlement. "What dirty jokes?"

Soon the kitchen was all cleaned up. The dishes were dried and put away, the kitchen table cleared off, the floor swept.

"Come on, Mama," Eddy called out. "Time for the tree trimming!"

The back door opened, and Maria's parents came in, with much stamping of snow. "I'll go to church with you tonight," Nonna said, as they all kissed her and wished her a Merry Christmas.

"You going to church tonight, Nonno?" Gianna asked her grandfather.

The little old man shrugged his shoulders and

smiled, a twinkle in his dark eyes. "I go if Cesare goes."

Maria laughed. "Now that's what I call being on the safe side."

"I don't know, Mama," Rose said, taking off her apron. "With all the wine Papa's had today I think he'd go to Jerusalem tonight."

The doorbell rang. Cesare called out, "Rose, your boyfriend's here!"

The living room was a shambles, with boxes and cartons strewn all over the floor amid pine needles and tissue paper.

"When I think of the hours we spent cleaning and polishing in here," Maria remarked ruefully.

"Okay, everybody grab some ornaments," Cesare said.

But Julio, the orderly one, put up his hands. "Whoa, Papa."

"Don't you whoa me like a horse. I'm your father. Don't you forget."

"But wait. There are too many of us. We can't all get around the tree at the same time. We'll take turns. That's it. We'll have shifts."

Cesare dipped his hand into a box and pulled out a shining red ball. "Well, okay, I put the first one," he said with a flourish. "You know why? Because I'm A-1 kid, that's why."

"Here we go again," Maria murmured under her breath.

The tree was trimmed. It stood beautiful and elegant

in front of the curtained windows, with softly shining colored lights glowing on bright ornaments and gaudy tinsel.

Julio said, "Well, Papa, you get to put the final touch. As A-1 father of this house."

Cesare, cigar in his mouth, took the white-and-gold angel from its crumbling cardboard box, handling it with a strange gentleness as if it might turn to dust if touched too roughly.

It was well worn by now. The edges were frayed, and the angel's hair was yellowed with age.

"You see what it says on the back? 'To Maria from Cesare. Christmas, 1914.' "

He placed the angel on the very top of the tree, and then, in a moment of romantic nostalgia, he bent over his wife and kissed her.

"You see? I'm still A-1 lover boy besides."

And Maria had to laugh at him, but she didn't kiss him back. She had been taught that a woman didn't show affection for her husband in front of others.

Gianna saw the look that passed between her mother and grandmother and sensed what they were thinking: It had turned out well, this arranged marriage to the fiercely handsome young immigrant from Bari.

The gifts were gathered from different parts of the house and arranged under the tree. They were small, inexpensive presents, mostly handmade, but to be given with such love that their value was beyond price.

As they were handed out, one at a time, Gianna

curled up on the floor beside the oil burner and wished she could hold this night forever. And she wondered what it would be like on some other Christmas Eve in the future, when the girls would be bringing their husbands and children home for the tree trimming. And Julio would be a doctor and Eddy a lawyer, and she, Gianna, would be an archaeologist, perhaps just returned from an expedition in Africa or South America.

But for now it was enough just to have this Christmas Eve in all its beauty and perfection. The lights of the tree cast soft, shimmering shadows on the smiling faces of her grandparents. The flames glowed, bright and orange, behind the isinglass window of the oil burner, while in the night outside the gentle snowfall was slowly turning into a major winter storm.

6

After the long bitter winter, spring was finally in the air. The elms in Columbus Park were budding, the lawns newly green. There was a lightness in people's footsteps, a new sparkle in their eyes, a stirring of old dreams. For the poor spring was something to be welcomed after the hardships of winter.

But for the Dellesantos this particular spring held sadness, for Nonna was dying.

The exact cause of her illness was treated as a dark secret, never openly discussed, but once Gianna caught the word "malignancy" in a conversation overheard between her parents and realized it was cancer.

Nonna knew she was dying, despite all the reassurances of her family that her illness was only the strain of old age. It was something she accepted rather than lamented, for she was in her seventies and could not live forever. She had done her share for posterity. She had raised seven children of her own, and two adopted ones, and was grandmother and great-grandmother to a number of other children. In her own mind she was content that her time had come, but she was angered by the sudden frenzy that arose as to where she should die, in whose house, at whose nursing.

At the first realization of what lay ahead her three

daughters had wanted to take her into their homes, but she had been determined to stay in her own house, surrounded by her own walls, her own belongings, her own memories. And so they had worked out a system of caring for her, of taking turns spending time with her during the days, staying over in the nights.

And when Gianna came to see her on a fresh green day in late April, her mother met her at the kitchen door and gently told her that her grandmother had just died.

Gianna looked slowly around the kitchen, at the dull cream-colored walls, the starched polka-dot curtains at the windows, the huge china closet with the good dishes and glassware standing in neat rows on paper doilies. She thought back to all the years she had come up here as a child, and Nonna had made her coffee and given her pastry or cookies. She had loved her grandmother. There were two generations between them, and they lived in different worlds, for Nonna had never really left the old country. Yet there had been the strong warm bond of love between them, the frequent exchanges of advice, of philosophy, of nostalgia.

She has taken a part of my life with her, Gianna thought, something I'll never know again.

Her mother gave her a cup of coffee, and Gianna wept as she drank it.

"Why do you cry?" her mother asked. "She was old and sick, and now she will no longer suffer, she will be with God."

"I'll miss her, Mama."

"Of course you will. We all will. But this is life, Gianna. We spend our lives dying a little each day."

Zio Luigi came from the bedroom, his dark face streaked with tears. He walked over to the window and stared out at the tiny patch of spring sky beyond the dress factory, and said in a broken voice, "I'll give her the best funeral money can buy. The neighborhood will talk about it for the rest of their lives, the funeral she had."

The wake was a big event in the neighborhood. Wakes were usually held in the home. To be laid out in a funeral parlor signified one of two things: a condition of secret wealth or an attitude of indecent extravagance.

Gianna would always remember that wake. Death conjured up all sorts of wild visions of purgatory and hell and the uncertain delights of a paradise not easily attained. The soul in purgatory was a thing of terrifying suffering. And it must stay there for years and years, because weren't the sisters and the priest always saying that if you said this prayer you would have so many years taken off your stay in purgatory, and if you did such and such a thing you would have so many more years taken off? Purgatory seemed like a bottomless, endless pit of agonized waiting. She hoped Nonna wouldn't be there too long.

At the funeral parlor Nonno sat nearest to the casket, a small, bewildered-looking man who seemed already lost without his wife. Next to him sat Zia Louisa, Zia Rosa from New York, and then Maria, all dressed in black from head to foot, clutching damp handkerchiefs with which they frequently dried their tears. Cesare and the uncles spent most of the time clustered in small groups in the hall, or smoking outside in the cool spring air.

Gianna sat still and pale between Rose and Annamarie in the first row of folding chairs reserved for the family.

But the dominating figure of all this was Nonna herself. She looked quite impressive in the gleaming bronze casket Zio Luigi had selected and paid for. She wore a new black dress with lace trimming and pearls at her throat. Her rosary beads were entwined in her thick, waxlike hands. There was a stern, tight expression on her thin lips, as if she were disapproving of the whole thing. It seemed to Gianna that at any moment she would bolt up out of her expensive coffin and say, "What nonsense! All this money could have been in my bankbooks instead!"

Most of the neighborhood people came as soon as the hour of the wake began and stayed until the funeral parlor closed for the night. It was like opening night, Gianna thought later, and no one wanted to miss any of the acts.

They sat in whispering groups, the women in their "good" black dresses, the young girls in their best clothes, and the men in the dark suits they wore for weddings and funerals. All had known the woman who lay in the casket. She had actually meant nothing to them in their daily struggle to exist, but she was one of them and deserved their last respect.

Once they had said their prayer at the coffin rail and blessed themselves, squeezed the hands of the husband and the women mourners, and wept a few tears, they settled down in their individual groups, and their whispering cut the silence.

"Did you see that casket? Did you ever expect her to have such a fine, expensive one?"

"The son must of paid for it."

"How much insurance you think she had?"

"Who knows? She saved pennies. She told me once she had three bankbooks."

"So, what's three bankbooks? You could have one dollar in each one."

"But she had her property."

"Look at the old man. How many times I heard him singing in the cellar with his *comparo.* They would go down and drink the wine when she went out for awhile. Well, the old man can drink the wine all day now, she won't come home to stop him."

"Look how the son grieves. He should be ashamed to come, all the disgrace he brought to her. They shouldn't allow him to even step inside a decent wake."

"Well, he's her son. Can you pick your children? You take them as they come, the good with the bad."

"I wonder if his friends will come."

But it was a disappointingly uneventful evening. The priest came in and said the rosary, and everyone joined in the responses. The well-corseted, black-dressed women in their whispering groups had expected something more. It was just an ordinary wake after all. Silence settled over the funeral parlor.

Until eight-thirty. Then there was a stirring of excitement, a new flurry of whispering.

"*Marrone,* look who's coming in!"

At the back of the room four men were extending condolences to Zio Luigi, and Gianna recognized them as his business partners. At least that was what Cesare had called them in a sarcastic tone of voice when he pointed them out to her and her sisters at different times.

"You don't go near them," he warned, just as he always warned against their going to Luigi's house. Whenever Gianna asked why, he became angry.

"Never you mind why. You just listen to your father. He knows."

Maria was no help either. Luigi was her own brother, whom she had loved as a child, and whom she still loved. But at the mention of his name a shadow of pain would darken her eyes and her lips would tighten grimly.

"It's a long story," Maria would say, and turn away.

"I know what it is," Annamarie said once. "I'll bet he's in—" But she broke off when Maria rounded on her, furious.

The men strode briskly down the aisle between the rows of folding chairs. There was something frightening in the cold meanness of their faces, perhaps even a glimmer of satisfaction at the obvious anger and distress they saw in the mourners' eyes.

The men glanced at the dead woman, crossed themselves quickly, and dropped white envelopes into the plate near the casket. Then they pressed Nonno's hand and passed on to console the women mourners.

Gianna looked back at Luigi and saw him whispering to a pretty blonde girl who was standing at the half-open door.

She's the one, Gianna thought. She's the one who lives with him.

It was just like a James Cagney movie. For the moment she could even forget her grief over her grandmother's death.

She watched the men leave as quickly and silently as they had come. The people from the neighborhood were satisfied. It had been a good wake after all.

The last friend and neighbor had gone home, and now only the immediate family remained in Cesare's kitchen. The big table was littered with ashtrays, empty glasses, trays of cookies and pastry, and bottles of whiskey and anisette.

The aunts were boiling over with fury, their grief forgotten for the moment.

"Did you see them?" Zia Louisa shouted, her huge bosom heaving beneath her black dress. "They walked in there as if they owned the place."

Her husband laughed. "As a matter of fact, one of them does have part interest in it."

"And that blonde! To think all our friends and

neighbors were there, and for years they can talk about Maria Delmonico's wake."

Zia Louisa began to cry noisily. "Oh, poor, poor Mama! How she must be turning over in her grave."

Cesare snorted. "What grave? She's still at the funeral parlor!"

And then all the women began to weep, and they talked of old times, and remembered the days when they were all young, and then they remembered that some day they, too, would die, and that made them weep all the more.

7

It was June, and already the heat slapped the pavements and warmed away the dampness of tenement walls. Life returned to the neighborhood. During the winter people seldom saw each other, except at Mass, or at Rizzuti's Meat Market, or Santini's Fresh Poultry. Now, suddenly, each person's life belonged to the neighbors. There were few secrets in the summertime, when romances and family quarrels and hopes and dreams drifted through the open windows of the tenements and were later discussed on the front stoops.

But it was the best time of the year. For it was a time of laughter, a time of sharing.

Gianna sat on the front steps with a *National Geographic* in one hand and in the other a heel of Italian bread drenched with olive oil. She tried to read, but the voices of the women on the stoop next door carried loud and harsh on the evening breeze and interfered with her concentration.

They gathered there every night, just as women and children gathered on the other stoops of the neighborhood on summer evenings. Sometimes their voices were low and hushed as they discussed the certain goings-on of the unmarried girl across the way, and sometimes strident as when they complained about their own various misfortunes.

"Gianna!" Mrs. Apuzzo called out. "Where's your mother?"

"She's getting ready for tomorrow, Mrs. Apuzzo. We're going to Julio's graduation in Boston."

The women smiled, fat arms crossed on voluminous breasts. "Everybody's graduating in your family this month."

"Not everybody. Just three!"

Mrs. Apuzzo threw up her arms. "Three's enough at one time!"

Gianna leaned back against the railing and breathed in deeply of the cool evening air. Happiness flooded her, excitement ran wild in her. Oh, God, she thought, you are making all the dreams come true.

Tomorrow Julio would graduate and go on to medical school on a partial scholarship. Rose was graduating from teachers' college next week, and Paolo from high school the week after.

Paolo, the future priest! She sometimes wondered if he really would have thought about being a priest if her mother hadn't pushed him into it.

Why did a mother want a son to be a priest? Once she had asked Maria, and Maria had said softly, "Every Catholic mother dreams of a son being a priest. Then she knows she has given God a special gift."

Gianna could hardly wait until she would graduate from grammar school next year and start high school.

High school! She would say the words over and over to herself. Rose and Annamarie had told her how exciting it was to get away from parochial school and the fierce, silent discipline of the nuns. And there would be a whole new world opening up to her, a world beyond Grand Avenue and Wooster Street. And a different kind of people.

A new world. A new life. But another year to wait.

Right now she was looking forward to Rose's wedding. Annamarie would be maid of honor, and Gianna and Rose's girlfriend May would be bridesmaids. They had been working on the gowns. Maria had more time now that Cesare had made her give up the job in the sweatshop.

He had never approved of her going back to work. It was a sharp blow to his masculine pride, particularly when he saw how exhausted and irritable she was at the end of the day. After a few months he had given her an ultimatum: either she quit the job or he would tell her boss to fire her. Maria quit, gladly.

Annamarie called from the doorway, "Gianna, come in!"

In the kitchen Guy Lombardo's music flowed forth from the little radio on the sewing machine. Rose was pouring coffee, and Maria set the bottle of anisette on the table.

Cesare lifted his coffee cup. "To all the graduates!" He added some anisette, then asked, "Where's the priest tonight?"

"Working," Maria said.

He shrugged. "Well, he's got the summer to live the worldly life."

"Cesare!" Maria reproached him. She didn't like it when he joked about Paolo's becoming a priest.

"What's a matter? A man can't make a joke in his own house? He has to go someplace else?"

"You don't joke about someone becoming a priest."

"You know, that's the trouble with your family. Nobody laughs about nothing. Nobody ever makes a joke." He winked at his daughters. "Don't I always tell you, my side of the family has all the good nature?"

"Only one thing bothers me about Paolo becoming a priest," Maria said with a faint smile. "You'll have to go to confession before having him give you communion when he says his first Mass."

Silently Cesare shared her apprehensions.

"The confession of all time," Maria went on, as if testing his good humor. "When you go to that confession they will have to hire another priest because it will take you so long to tell it. And they will have to keep the church open all night so you'll have enough time to do your penance."

Cesare's good humor seemed suddenly to have disappeared. "All right, all right."

"Well, this is a time to celebrate, not to fight. We must all go to bed early because tomorrow will be a big day. You're sure Leonardo's going to be here on time?"

"Of course! You think he's a dummy?"

"Are you sure his car will go that far?" Rose asked apprehensively. "From what I remember it didn't look as if it would go around the block."

"Listen. When my *comparo* says his car will take us, it will take us. We have his word."

"Some word," Maria muttered. "He was probably full of wine when he said it."

Cesare shrugged airily. "You stand in good with God. You put in a word tonight when you say your prayers, that's all."

Maria had let Zia Louisa have the door key, and when they returned from the graduation the house was full of aunts and uncles and cousins, even the divorced cousin with his new wife. And the air was rich with the fragrance of rum cake and fresh-perked coffee.

Zia Louisa met them at the door, and hugged Julio affectionately. "Congratulations! Dr. Dellesanto!"

He pulled away, laughing. "I'm not a doctor yet."

It was while they were having a second round of coffee that Zia Louisa had some news about Nonno.

"Papa's going back to Italy for a visit."

"Good!" Cesare said, helping himself to a Sicilian *cannoli,* the tubular pastry filled with ricotta cream. "It's about time he had some fun out of life."

"Cesare!" Maria chided him, frowning.

"So what you expect? He should climb in the coffin with the old lady? So he goes to the old country and has a good time. So what's wrong with that?"

Zia Louisa shrugged. "Nothing. So long as he don't spend all the money."

"The money, the money. Who cares what money he spends?"

"He has to think of the future."

At this Cesare howled. "The future! The man's seventy-five years old. What does he care about the future?"

"Where is he tonight?" Maria asked her sister.

"He didn't feel too well. If you ask me, he's been sampling too much wine in the cellar since Mama died. At least when she was living she would keep track. I don't have time to keep an eye on the wine barrel. I told him to come live with me, but he says he has to live in his own house. I do the best I can. I clean the house for him, I cook his food, I wash his clothes. What more can I do?"

"When's he going?"

"Next week. Can you imagine? Papa going to the old country at seventy-five years of age? He can't even find his way downtown, so he's got to cross the ocean."

"Well, I guess he can't get lost on a boat."

"Boat! He's going part of the way by plane. He's going to Paris and then flying to Rome!"

Everyone laughed now. The idea of dear old Nonno taking a plane by himself was too much to take seriously.

"Maybe it's just as well," Zia Louisa went on.

"We'll see him off. Someone will meet him in Rome. He can't get lost too easily, I guess."

Gianna lay awake in the darkness. Rose and Annamarie were already asleep, but Gianna wasn't even tired. She remembered every detail of this exciting day.

It had started out hot and sunny.

"I'm glad," Maria said, pouring out coffee for breakfast. "It will be a nice day for a long drive."

"If the car goes all right," Rose said.

Cesare glowered at her. "What you mean, if the car goes? You think she won't go?"

"I hope it does, Papa. I sure don't want to get stuck somewhere."

Maria crossed herself. "God forbid!" She looked darkly at her husband. "We'd better not miss that graduation, that's all I can say. I've waited too many years for this day to miss the biggest event. We could have taken the train and been sure of getting there all right."

Cesare exploded. "We don't leave the house yet and already you've missed the graduation!"

God must indeed have watched over them, for despite two flat tires, a noisy muffler, and a near accident, the Dellesantos arrived at the college in the middle of the afternoon. Julio and Eddy met them and took them on a tour of the grounds. And then Cesare took them to an elegant Italian restaurant for dinner. It was the first time in her life that Gianna had ever been to a restaurant.

But the best part was seeing Julio walk down the aisle, tall and good looking in his black gown and cap. Gianna would always remember the way her mother and father looked when Julio smiled at them as he passed, a look of pride and happiness.

Gianna smiled too, in the darkness, and decided to go downstairs for a glass of cold water. She hesitated in the living room when she heard her father and Paolo talking in the kitchen. She took another step and could see them sitting at the table.

"Well, pretty soon will be your turn to go away," her father was saying.

"Yes, pretty soon, Papa," Paolo agreed.

Cesare put down his cigar. He leaned over and grasped his son's hand. "Paolo, are you sure?"

"Sure about what, Papa?"

"You know what I mean. About being a priest."

"Nobody's forcing me, Papa. It's my own choosing. Why do you keep asking me?"

"Because sometimes I don't know if you choose, or your mother, she choose. I think you don't really know your mind yet."

Paolo looked down at the table. "I have to find out for myself, Papa. No one can help me in this. But I will have lots of time to find out. It's not as if I have to decide right away. All I know is that I have to find out for sure, or else I shall go through all my life not knowing."

Cesare sighed heavily. "Well, maybe so. A man has to find his own way, that's true. Only—only I want you to know something from me. It don't make a difference to me if you become a priest or don't become a priest. It's your mother who wants it. Me, I'm your father, I'm a man. I know what it is to be a man. I can understand if you tell me, 'Papa, I've changed my mind, I want to be something else.' You understand what I say?"

Paolo looked at his father and smiled. "I understand, Papa. And I promise you I'll give it up if I don't think it's right for me. If I'm going to be a priest, I have to be a good one."

Gianna turned and went back upstairs. She would get her drink from the bathroom sink. As she waited for the water to run a little colder, she thought that pretty soon only she and Annamarie would be at home. And then it would be their turn. What would it be like here when they had all left? What would the house be like then, without the constant excitement of schools and students and ambitions and dreams?

On the morning of the wedding Gianna woke before the others. It was only six o'clock, and the room was cool and shadowy. She looked over at Rose, sleeping on a cot because Valerie had her bed, and thought a little wistfully that this was the last morning Rose would be sleeping in this room. Tomorrow morning she would awaken in another bed in another city and Mario would be lying there beside her. She would have a new name and be a new person, and her life would never be the same again.

"And wish you were single again," Zia Louisa had often teased, hinting of dark mysteries in married life.

Gianna looked then at Valerie, whom Julio had brought home for the first time. Valerie Courtney with her ash-blonde hair and violet-blue eyes and fair skin. And Gianna remembered Cesare's face when Julio introduced them.

In Cesare's eyes there had been a touch of wistfulness, as if in this girl, so obviously a stranger to his own world, he was seeing for the first time that by educating his children he was actually sending them away from him. Naively he had believed that someday Julio would return to New Haven and settle down with a nice Italian girl. Now there was the possibility that Julio would never come back here to live, that he would remain in Boston and become a part of Valerie Courtney's world.

Maria came into the bedroom, still in her nightgown and old cotton robe. "Good morning, girls. This is the big day."

"Good morning, Mama."

Rose said, "Mama, come sit down. Let's talk for a few minutes."

Maria sat on the edge of the cot, and Rose took her hand.

"Mama, I want you to know that I was very happy growing up here. It was a beautiful life."

Maria wiped her eyes. "It was a hard life. We had nothing to give you."

"No, Mama, you're wrong. It was a rich, wonderful life. You and Papa—and my brothers and sisters—gave me something all the money in the world couldn't buy. You gave me your love and dreams, and that will carry me through my whole life no matter what happens to me."

Maria threw her arms around Rose and held her close for a moment, silently. Gianna and Annamarie, also caught up in the tide of emotion, climbed upon the cot and joined in the embrace.

Rose broke away from them, laughing, her face wet. "Hey, this isn't a funeral, this is my wedding day! What are we all weeping for?"

"Because we'll miss you!" Gianna cried.

A lusty shout rang through the house. "Maria!"

"Mother of God," Maria muttered. She looked over at Rose. "I only hope your husband will have a better disposition than your father. That man will give me heart failure one of these days."

She hurried away to find out what Cesare was shouting about.

Eddy sang "Here Comes the Bride" as Rose came down the stairs in her wedding gown. The shimmering white satin fell softly in a long skirt and train, and the seeded pearl tiara atop her long dark hair gave her a look of royalty. Her olive skin glowed, her brown eyes sparkled with happiness.

Cesare reached out for her and held her at arms' length. "Like a queen," he murmured proudly. "A queen never looked more beautiful."

She kissed him. "Thanks, Papa. You look pretty handsome yourself."

He straightened the black bow tie of his tuxedo. "But of course! To give away a queen a man has to look like a king, right?" He proudly surveyed his other two daughters in their flowing gowns of pink and blue tulle. "Mama mia, how can one man bring so many beautiful daughters into the world?"

Maria laughed. "Yes, you did it all yourself. I wasn't even there. When they're good and beautiful, they're your children. When they're bad, they're mine."

"My children, they're always good and beautiful," Cesare said.

Maria cautioned, "Look, this is your daughter's wedding day and I think you've already had too much wine."

He glowered at her. "Look, just because it's a special day don't take no liberty with me. Just because I'm in a good mood and got a chance to kiss all the pretty girls, don't you get jealous. Remember, you're still *Numero Uno.* These others"—he waved a generous hand toward the smiling girls—"they are only the appetizers."

He laughed at his sons, who were watching him in tolerant amusement, hoping for the best since this was only nine-thirty in the morning and there was still a long day ahead. "How's that for words, eh? Maybe your father, he don't go to college like you, but don't kid yourself, he's A-1 kid!"

"Speaking of weddings," Annamarie said, as they prepared to leave for the church, "you know who eloped?"

"No. Who?" her mother asked.

"Laura Riccitelli."

Instinctively Gianna looked at Paolo and saw in his dark eyes a sudden sadness that startled her.

"Who did she marry?"

"I don't know. Nobody around here. A sailor, I think."

The reception was in full swing. Gianna, dancing with Eddy, said, "It really was a lovely wedding, wasn't it?"

"Yes, Rose made a beautiful bride. Some day you'll be a bride, too, Gianna. And just as beautiful."

She laughed at him. "I won't be a bride for years and years. And then some." She felt proud to be dancing with this brother that she so loved.

"Do you have a special girl, Eddy?"

"Me!" His dark eyes danced. "I have too many things to do first before I settle down. Besides, why should I make one girl happy when I can make them all delirious? Anyway, I have two more years of college, and then law school."

"Julio has a long way to go, too," she said, watching her oldest brother and Valerie dance by.

"Well, he met the right girl. Maybe I will, too, before I get through school. You never know. And how about you, little sister? You're really growing up, you know? Next year high school, right?"

She sighed. "Yes, but it seems so far away."

"So far away? What's the great hurry?"

"I hate grammar school. I feel like I outgrew it long ago."

His face turned serious for a moment. "Don't wish your life away. Enjoy every minute of it as you go along. You see, every year of your life has a special meaning, and when you wish it away you lose something you can never find again. It's gone forever. Hey, you still want to be an archaeologist?"

"That's right."

"Well, I always said that was what our family needed to give it real class. No, I'm only kidding. If when the time comes that's what you really want to do, then you go ahead and don't let anyone—not even Papa—talk you out of it."

"Even if I'm a girl?"

He laughed and hugged her. "Hey, who's that good-looking guy Annamarie's so cozy with?"

She followed his glance and saw her sister dancing with a dark-haired boy who was holding her close and whispering in her ear. "Oh, that's Leonardo's grandson, Sal Donato. He lives around the corner from us."

"Well, he sure seems to like her."

"Looks like it. Wouldn't Papa be happy about that?"

"Why?"

"He's a nice Italian boy."

Eddy laughed again. "Valerie's not Italian and Mama and Papa have accepted her quite well, it seems."

"That's because Julio's a son. Somehow I think they're more old fashioned when it comes to daughters. They sure were glad when Rose picked Mario."

Rose was ready to throw her bouquet. Eddy said to Gianna, "Aren't you going to try for it?"

"Why? I don't want to be the next bride. Remember? You said not to rush things."

They laughed and watched as the young, single girls gathered in a group. It was Annamarie who caught it.

Cesare gave her a violent hug. "The next bride. Only wait a few years, okay? Give us time to get over this wedding first."

Eddy said, "Well, little sister, I'm going to leave you

now. Julio has his Valerie, and Paolo isn't dancing. So that leaves only me to carry out the male obligation of the Dellesanto family to keep the single girls happy. Why don't you go talk to Paolo? He looks kind of left out of things. I don't know why. Just because he's going to be a priest doesn't mean he can't dance at his sister's wedding."

The music of the tarantella filled the great room. People of every age were on the floor now, even the old and the very young. Flushed faces and breathless voices, happy shouts, twirling arms and kicking legs, all dancing with gay abandon.

Gianna made her way to where Paolo was standing at the edge of the dance floor alone. She remembered the sadness on his face when Annamarie told them that Laura Riccitelli was married.

She touched his arm. "Come on, Paolo, dance with me."

He shook his head. "I'm not a dancer."

"Neither am I. Come on. All you have to do is kick your legs and move around fast."

He smiled then, and she pulled him into the crowd and soon had him laughing.

The conductor was calling out for the passengers to board the train.

"And send us a card as soon as you get there," Maria was telling Rose.

"I will, Mama, and stop crying. I'm going on my honeymoon, not to my funeral."

"It's almost the same thing," Zia Louisa muttered in the background, her face flushed from too much vermouth.

Everyone laughed then, and Cesare put his arm around Rose and kissed her. He looked at her new husband and warned, "You take good care of my daughter."

Mario smiled lovingly at Rose. "You don't have to worry about that, Papa."

Cesare beamed. "Papa! Everybody, you hear that? Only married one day and already he calls me Papa. I have children all over the place." He turned to Maria. "Well, Mama, our first wedding. One down and five more to go." He remembered Paolo and corrected himself. "Excuse me, four to go."

Only Eddy saw the tears in Gianna's eyes. He squeezed her shoulder and murmured, "Why the tears? This is a happy day."

She rubbed a hand across her eyes. "I was just thinking it's sort of a milestone in our lives. You know, Rose will have her own life now. It will never again be like it was before."

"Nothing stays the same forever, little sister."

"I know. Only—only sometimes you wish it could."

"Just think of the bonus in having Rose get married."

"Bonus?"

"You'll have your own bed for the first time in your life!" He looked over at Annamarie, whose face was aglow as Sal Donato whispered something in her ear.

"Who knows? You may even have your own room before too long!"

The train pulled away from the platform, slowly, noisily. With Mario at her side, Rose waved from the dusty window, smiling as she set forth on her new venture, the orchid on her beige suit a proud declaration to the world that she was a brand-new bride.

Gianna remembered all the years Rose had shared her life and been sister and friend and second mother to her. And then the sadness passed, and Gianna's heart was filled with joy and anticipation.

One day I, too, will be going away, leaving Mama and Papa and the family behind me, she thought. I, too, will have dreams of my own to fulfill.

The train taking her sister off to the beginning of a new life faded out of sight. Gianna looked around her at the family she loved so dearly and knew that indeed it was possible for all dreams to come true.

PART II

And New Beginnings

1941-1943

9

An icy wind rattled the windows and made a bold clean sweep of the darkened bedroom. Gianna glanced over at the calendar on the bureau. Sunday, December 7, 1941. She snuggled under the blankets in delicious laziness. How she loved Sundays now that her life was so busy, especially since she had started to work after school and on Saturdays in a bookstore with Annamarie.

Annamarie was still asleep, her beautiful black hair spread out on the white pillowcase. After only one year of business school, Annamarie had dropped out to accept a job as manager of the Book Shoppe. Cesare and Maria had not tried to change her mind. After all, they reasoned to themselves privately, one of these days she would marry Sal Donato. She had been going with him ever since Rose's wedding. A few times Annamarie had gone out with someone else in the neighborhood, but nothing ever came of those dates. She always returned to Sal. He was always there, waiting for her.

Gianna slipped out of bed and wrapped her woolen robe around her. She went to the window and, lifting the shade, looked out on the December morning.

It was still half dark, bleak, dreary. The yard looked desolate with the grape vines cut down and the garden area brown. The fruit trees shivered nakedly in the wind, and beyond the wooden fence the dress factory was dark and silent, and forbidding, its grim windows glimmering eerily like many evil eyes in the shadows. To the left and right Gianna could see the tenements with their drawn shades, their brick walls cold and lonely looking. Here and there a solitary light broke the darkness.

Annamarie opened her eyes and yawned. "What time is it?"

"Seven-ten."

"What are you doing up so early?"

"I'm going to eight o'clock Mass."

"I'm not," said Annamarie, burrowing deeper into her blankets. "I'm meeting Sal for the eleven."

Rose and Mario came over to Sunday dinner, as they always did, and today Rose was radiant. "We have some wonderful news for you!" she announced when they had finished the pasta.

"You're going to have a baby!" Maria said delightedly.

She had waited for four years to become a grandmother. Whenever she broached the subject to Rose, her daughter laughed and said that first they must save up enough money for a house.

"What's all this about having to have a house before you can start a family?" Maria would demand to know.

"If people waited to have a house first years ago, nobody would ever have been born."

Rose would say with her new sophistication, "Well, it's different today, Mama. Today you don't have to start right out with a family."

"Don't tell me. All these new-fangled ideas. I suppose you're lucky times have changed. In my day you could expect to have a baby nine months after you were married. Well, just watch that after you get the house you don't say, 'Let's wait till we get some more furniture, let's wait till we have a big bank account.' All of a sudden you'll find yourself in the change of life and it'll be too late."

Rose was laughing now. "Oh, Mama, you have a one-track mind. No, it's not a baby. We just looked at a house, and it's beautiful. You'll love it. Wait till you see it, Papa, it even has fruit trees."

Cesare was quite pleased. "Another landowner in my family," he said, lighting a cigar. "Good! My father, he say to me when I leave the old country, 'Buy land, buy a house. Then you have something all your own. Some things change, but property is always valuable.' Never mind your mother, you're smart. Hurry up and finish dinner. I have to see this house."

There was a knock on the back door, and Zia Louisa rushed in like a dark tornado in her black Sunday dress, her face pale and distraught. She stared at their happy, smiling faces as they sat around the dinner table finishing up their coffee.

"What is it, Louisa?" Maria demanded. "You look like a ghost. Sit down here. Catch your breath. You want some coffee?"

Louisa shook her head violently, lowering her heavy bulk into a kitchen chair. "Didn't you have your radio on today? Don't you know what's happened?"

The smiles disappeared, the coffee cups were set down, there was a sudden, fearful silence at the table.

Gianna said, "We didn't have the radio on, Zia. What is it?"

"Pearl Harbor's been attacked by the Japs! It means war!"

A stunned silence now. Maria and Cesare stared at each other in sudden terror, a common fear reflected in their eyes. War—and they had sons. Strong, healthy sons.

Cesare left the table abruptly and turned on the radio. Grimly he listened to the tale of betrayal and death and chaos. To no one in particular he muttered, "You slave to make a better world for your sons. You work double shifts and sweat like a pig and break your back, and what good is it? A war comes along and where do all the dreams go then?"

Gianna went to him and slipped her arm around his shoulder. "Papa, don't worry. They won't touch Julio or Paolo. They probably won't take medical students or seminarians."

His tortured eyes burned into hers. "But I have another son," he said, almost in a whisper, "and he will be eligible."

Rose sat beside Mario, ashen faced, and slipped her hand into his. "Here we were planning to buy a house and maybe—maybe you'll have to go, too."

He squeezed her shoulder. "Let's not think that far ahead. We'll just take a day at a time."

But nonetheless the magical happiness of the day had been lost for all of them. There was nothing now but the bleak, fearsome shadow that had shut out all the joy.

It was only a week later that Eddy called and told them he had enlisted in the Air Force. Cesare slumped down at the kitchen table. "Why? Why did he have to rush it? Why couldn't he wait?"

Gianna said, "He did what he felt was right, Papa. He did what he thought he had to do."

Cesare raised clenched fists as in anger against an unseen enemy. "What he thinks is right? To throw up everything just like that? He couldn't wait till he got called?"

"It's better than being in the infantry, I guess. It's his life, Papa."

"Look who's telling me whose life it is."

"Papa, he's old enough to make his own decisions! They will take him anyway, one way or the other."

He brushed his hand across his eyes. "For this I had to work and dream. For this!"

10

It was the beginning of August, 1942, pleasantly warm and slightly breezy. The sunshine made golden shadows in the leaves of the elms and the grass of Columbus Park, and the sky was brilliantly blue.

A Sunday afternoon in August, like most Sunday afternoons in August, but different in a terrible way. It was the last day of her brother's leave before he expected to go overseas, and Gianna ached with the anguish and desolation.

Sitting beside Eddy on the park bench, she looked at him and saw how handsome he was in his Air Force uniform, tall and broad shouldered, his dark eyes gleaming in the tanness of his face.

There is nothing to worry about, she tried to reassure herself. He will come back. The war will end quickly and he will be home as if it never happened.

He had been home for five days, and everyone in the family had come to see him—aunts, uncles, cousins. Julio and Valerie drove down from Boston for the weekend, bringing Paolo with them. Julio had graduated from medical school in June and was now interning at a hospital in Boston. He and Valerie had been married a few months before by the Catholic chaplain at the medical school.

There had been a Sunday dinner like the old days, all of them together. When Eddy had his fill of lasagna, chicken baked with garlic and parsley, fruit, Italian pastry, and demitasse, he pushed his chair away from the table and groaned. "Mama, I won't be able to eat for another week."

His mother beamed with pleasure. "From what you told us about the food at camp you won't miss nothing."

"Mama, if you tasted the cook's lasagna—" Eddy turned to look at Rose in her maternity dress. "You're really blooming, big sister. I wish you had planned it better, though."

"What do you mean—planned it better?"

"By the time I get back the kid won't be a baby any more." Then, seeing the sudden shadow pass across the faces of his parents, he laughed. "I was only kidding. I'll be back in no time."

"Listen," Rose said lightly, "if it's a boy I just might stick your name in there somewhere."

Cesare glared at her. "If it's a boy you better stick my name in there somewhere, too."

Rose put her hands to her head in a mock gesture of despair. "What did I start here? Everybody who wants the baby named after them form a line to the right. And to think I had such great names in mind, too."

"What's a matter with my name?" Cesare demanded. "It's not good enough for you college people?"

"I didn't say that, Papa. But let's face it. A boy

named Cesare would have an awful lot to live up to."

Cesare beamed proudly. "You betcha your life!"

Eddy's voice brought Gianna back to the present. "Remember that school, Gianna?"

She looked over at the parochial school across from Columbus Park. It was empty and still on a Sunday afternoon in August.

"I think the thing I remember most about it," Eddy went on, "was the silence, the way they wouldn't let us talk in between classes or on the way out. Everyone was so quiet walking to the corner. Remember? Then the minute the nuns left us the boys were throwing chestnuts or snowballs at the girls or beating each other up. Remember?"

He was trying to make her laugh. She did manage a smile.

"By the time I get home from the war you will be really grown up."

"What do you think I am now? I'm seventeen!"

"Yes, and before you know it you'll be going off to college."

"Everyone else says I'm crazy to think about archaeology."

"Listen, you be what you want to be. If you change your mind in the meantime, that's something else. There's nothing wrong with that either. You know how many times I changed mine? I didn't always want to be a lawyer. I had a few other things in mind, too."

"Like what?"

"Oh, the FBI, an accountant, a garbage collector."

She laughed. "Oh, Eddy."

"I have a secret for you," Eddy said, his dark eyes shining. "I have a girl, Gianna."

He took a picture from his wallet. "Her name is Terry. Short for Teresa. You won't believe this, but she's Italian."

Looking at the snapshot of Eddy's pretty, dark-haired girl, Gianna said, "Mama and Papa would sure be happy to hear that. But why is it a secret?"

"Well, if I had told them they would have expected me to bring her home, and they would have made a big fuss over her, and somehow I wanted this leave to be just family. Besides, Terry and I haven't known each other too long. Maybe when the war is over we won't even feel the same as we do now. Lots of people will rush into marriage because of the war, and then when it's over they'll be strangers and maybe won't even like each other any more. No, we'd rather wait and be sure."

His eyes clouded over, as he lit a cigarette. "Thank God when this war is over and we can all lead normal lives again."

"Did you have to enlist? Couldn't you have waited?"

"For what? To be drafted? Like Sal? He was one of the first to have his number called. And he wound up in the infantry. No, it's better this way." He sighed. "Maybe Rose is lucky Mario is 4-F. A heart murmur's nothing much."

"I guess she's secretly glad, although Mario has mixed feelings about it. On one side he's glad because of the baby coming. But on the other he's kind of frustrated. People are always asking him when he's going. It's embarrassing to have to keep saying you're 4-F. People who have someone overseas don't look too kindly on 4-F's or deferments. Mama gets snide remarks sometimes about Julio and Paolo."

Eddy glanced down at his watch. "I think we'd better be getting back home."

They walked slowly through the park. When they came to the church she stopped and turned to him. "Would you mind if we went in for a minute? Even though we did go to Mass this morning?"

She thought he might laugh, but he didn't. Instead, he took her arm and together they went into the cool, shadowy stillness.

"Little sister," he murmured, "I need all the extra prayers I can get."

"I want to light a candle. Have you got any change on you? I didn't bring any."

"Sure. Here."

He knelt with her as she lit the taper and a tiny flame began to flicker in the red glass holder.

Bring him back safely, she prayed. Don't let anything happen to him.

Gianna, Julio, and Annamarie were the only ones who went to the station with Eddy. "I couldn't bear to look back and see the whole family standing there," he said.

Gianna could understand why. It was hard enough to say good-bye at home, with Maria crying and hugging him constantly, and Cesare red eyed, his voice shaking. Even Rose, who was always so calm and controlled, started to cry.

"Don't forget," Eddy teased, "when you have the baby, stick my name in there somewhere. Only if it's a boy, of course."

Rose laughed shakily. "You can count on it. I promise."

"Poor kid, he'll probably wind up with half a dozen names."

He squeezed Paolo's hand. "Paolo, you say some extra prayers for me."

Then he turned to his parents and hugged them, trying not to cry with them. "And don't you worry about me, Mama, Papa. I'll be fine. Don't you remember what that fortune-teller told you once about me, Mama? She said I'd lead a charmed life. So don't worry. And listen, once I get there—wherever it is—we'll just finish that war so fast—" His voice broke then. "Just don't worry. Okay?"

They held onto him as if they'd never let him go.

The railroad platform was crowded with other servicemen being seen off by their families and girlfriends and wives. The train pulled in and the men began to board it. There were good-byes and tears and embraces, and no one wanting the train to leave.

"Well, this is it," Eddy said.

He grasped Julio's hand and held it tightly. "Don't forget, you're the big brother, Doctor. You check up on these pretty sisters of ours. Make sure the Marines and sailors don't take advantage of them. And keep a check on the parents, too—you know? They're taking all this pretty hard."

"Sure, Eddy. I'll do all I can to make it easier. Just be sure and write as often as you can. And take care of yourself."

Eddy hugged Annamarie. "You be a good girl and look after Mama and Papa. I'm depending on you. And you, too, little sister," he said, turning to Gianna, who threw her arms around him tearfully. "You make sure you keep up those marks. I expect you to get high honors this year. You hear me?"

She nodded, trying to smile.

The laughter was gone from his handsome face. At this last moment, unmasked, the reality was stark and sorrowful.

"So long for now," he said to them, his voice breaking, and he turned quickly and hurried up the steps of the last car.

It was as the train pulled away and she no longer saw his face at the dusty window that Gianna remembered something she had wanted to tell him. She was filled with desolation. Tears streamed down her cheeks.

Julio put an arm around her. "Come, Gianna, let's go home."

"I forgot to tell him—" she said, staring numbly at the empty tracks.

And she suddenly remembered so many things she had never told him. There had just never been enough time.

11

By September the grapes nestled in purple clusters in the cool green shadows of the arbor. September, and the air was still warm, although there were mornings and evenings when it felt like late autumn. In Columbus Park the trees were beginning to turn color.

As Gianna walked down the street with Annamarie, her books held snugly under her arm, she reflected on the changes 1942 had brought.

The war had touched everyone by now. In every family in the neighborhood there were sons, brothers, nephews, or husbands in the service. Already there was a gold star in the front window of a house across the street, and a grief-stricken mother who moved about in mourning clothes and hardly ever spoke to anyone.

The mailman was a friend, awaited twice a day, patiently and hopefully, but the Western Union man was looked on with terror. Whenever he was seen, a shadow of fear fell over the neighborhood, and there were sighs of relief when he passed by to another house.

There were changes in the everyday living. Rationing and shortages, pale oleomargarine instead of butter, dark shades or curtains on all windows, air-raid wardens patrolling the blocks at night to be sure lights were blacked out. War bonds in the theaters, USO dances and canteens, women standing in line for nylons. And the loneliness.

Gianna and Annamarie turned in at the front gate and walked around to the back of the house.

"Gianna, did you hear about Laura Riccitelli?"

"No. What about her?"

"Her husband deserted her. She's back home with her mother."

"That was a short marriage. I guess she had bad luck when she met that guy."

In the yard Cesare was inspecting the grapes as he did every day now, waiting almost impatiently for that moment when they would be just the perfect ripeness for the wine.

He wouldn't have any of the boys to help him this year. He would have to depend on Mario. They had all laughed about that. Mario had never made wine in his life.

"So you learn," Cesare told him. "I teach you."

"Hi, Papa!" the girls called out to him. Cesare waved, the sun shining in his thick red hair.

In the kitchen the sisters were greeted by the rich, pungent aroma of rice and beans, and coffee just beginning to perk. Maria, aproned and smiling, was waiting at the door.

"Supper will be ready in five minutes," she said.

Rose was sitting at the table. "Hi, girls, you have a guest tonight. Mario had a special dinner to go to, so I came to eat with you."

The doorbell rang. "I'll get it," Gianna said.

When she opened the front door and saw the grim-faced Western Union man, the world seemed to go topsy-turvy, spinning in whirling circles. She thought crazily, It's September and the grapes are big and purple and Eddy used to help Papa make the wine.

She heard her mother's and sisters' voices light and happy in the kitchen, and the smell of the rice and beans was rich and warm. She wanted to close the door so she would not see the telegram in the man's hand. If she closed the door he would go away.

"Who is it?" her mother called.

Gianna just stood there with the telegram in her hands. She looked around the room, at the familiar things of her everyday life, the crocheted chairback sets, the worn linoleum, her mother's knitting on the coffee table.

Her mother and sisters came into the room then, Maria wiping her hands on her apron. "Who was it?" she asked again.

Gianna handed her the telegram, and Maria read it. She sat down quickly on the sofa, her face pale. But she didn't cry. "He's dead, my Eddy's dead."

"Oh, Mama."

But still Maria didn't cry. She just sat there, looking suddenly very cold, her body trembling, her hands shaking. Silently the girls gathered around her and hugged her to them as if to warm her.

The back door opened, and there was the sound of Cesare in the kitchen, lifting the lid of the rice and beans. "Where is everybody? The rice is getting dried out!"

He came into the living room and saw them there, huddled close together, and then he saw the telegram on the coffee table. He read it and flung it to the floor.

"No!" he cried out in denial of the reality. "No, it's not true! It's a mistake. We find out. They make a mistake."

"They don't make mistakes, Papa, not about this," Annamarie said quietly.

The tears streamed down his cheeks. "Well, this is a mistake. We got a letter from him yesterday. Where's the letter?" Frantically he rummaged through the newspapers and magazines on the lamp table next to his chair. He pulled a thin piece of paper out from beneath a newspaper. "See? Here's the letter! He write it himself. Look what he says. I am fine, he says. See? Right here he says it himself."

Silence filled the shadows of the room.

He sank down into his chair and buried his face in his hands. "This is all it comes down to. You break your back, you sweat like a pig, you save and scrimp and sacrifice to give your children education, make them be something. You love them, you dream for them, you worry. And then—poof! In one second's time, in one piece of paper, it's all over, it was all for nothing. This is what it means to have children, to be a father, a mother."

Gianna went to him and wrapped her arms around him, weeping. "You still have the rest of us, Papa. There are still five of us left who love you and will make you happy and proud."

"What difference is it if I have twenty others? I lost my son. Does that change?"

"I know, Papa, I know."

He looked over at Maria and tenderness touched his face then. He went to her and his rough, calloused hands grasped hers and held them for a moment. He reached for words of consolation, but there were none, and then he turned from the room of sorrow, and the back door closed behind him.

Annamarie brought a cup of coffee and Maria drank it, still unable to cry, as if the tears were frozen deep inside her. She stared out the window, through the lace curtains, and she shared her memories with her daughters.

He was the best-behaved baby of the whole six, she said. He was so good-natured and happy, except when he was sick or teething. At those times she would put him in the old wooden cradle and rock it with her feet as she cooked, or as she scrubbed the clothes on the washboard in the sink.

When he was old enough to stand, she would wrap the lower part of him in a blanket, so that he was stiff like a board, then stand him in the open seat of a cane chair. He would stay like that for hours while he watched her iron and sew and clean house.

And as he grew up he seemed always to be conscious of her endless labors to make life good for the family. How many times he grabbed the mop from her and finished washing the kitchen floor.

"Someday, Mama," he would say laughingly, "someday when I'm a lawyer, I'm going to do so many things for you. You're going to enjoy life for once."

Someday. Lost forever.

But Gianna hardly heard her mother's words. She was remembering Eddy at Rose's wedding, so alive, whirling her across the crowded room while the orchestra played "Stardust" and all the pretty young girls watched her enviously.

She knew a longing to be near the things that had belonged to him. She went up to the boys' room and stood there in the shadows and her brother was still very much alive to her.

This room seemed to be awaiting his return. His law books were on the open shelves, and on the bureau was a bottle of after-shave lotion he had left behind. Fading sunlight made his basketball trophies gleam like silver.

Trophies for winning. He had always been a winner, but now he had lost the greatest tournament of all.

In the closet she found his favorite blue sports jacket, and she wrapped her arms around the emptiness of it.

Oh, my brother, my brother, my confidante, friend,

sharer of secrets, my fellow dreamer. I loved you so dearly, and there were so many things I wish I had told you, but there was never enough time.

She remembered her father then. She found him where she expected to find him, sitting on the bench under the grape arbor, his huge shoulders hunched over, sunlight, filtering through the grape leaves, resting on his bent red head.

She sat down beside him and slipped her hand into his. He turned and looked at her.

"He was a good boy, your brother. A good boy."

"Yes, Papa."

"You know what he used to say to me? Papa, someday when I'm a lawyer I take you and Mama to Italy myself. He used to always say it. So why did he have to be in such a hurry to get into the war?"

"He was a very brave man, Papa."

His eyes were filled with bitterness. "You think it means something to me that he was brave? Can I put my arms around his braveness? Will it be warm and loving like him?"

He rubbed his arm across his wet face. "What do I care now was he brave or not brave? All I know is my son is gone. That's all I know."

Cesare reached out and touched a cluster of grapes, and Gianna remembered with him those lost beautiful years. And the husky, black-eyed boy who cheerfully carried the huge wooden barrels up and down the cellar stairs, and whistled as he scrubbed them, never complaining that it was a hard, tedious job. And never complaining when his father made him carry the heavy, awkward jugs to *paisanos* in the neighborhood.

This year, Cesare said, he would not make the wine. Maybe he would never make it again. It would only make him remember those other years when his sons were small and they all worked together as he loved them and dreamed over them.

Cesare stood up. "Come, we go inside. Your mother, we go to her."

Just then Zia Louisa came hurrying breathlessly around the back of the house.

"I saw the Western Union man," she said. "I had to know."

"It's Eddy," Gianna said. "He's—he's been killed."

Her aunt crossed herself and sighed. "Damn this war. I have two sons overseas and one ready to go. And how many more will we lose before it's all over?"

She put her arm around Gianna and squeezed Cesare's hand. "Come inside."

After she had tried to console Maria and the girls, she said, "You haven't had supper yet, have you?"

"Who wants to eat?" Cesare asked, staring out the window.

"It's not what you want to do, it's what you have to do."

She went out to the kitchen and lifted the pot lid of the rice and beans. The pasty liquid had dried out, and the rice was all puffed up. She added a little hot water, gave a stir, and turned the gas on. A few minutes later she spooned out dishes and placed them on the table.

"Come," she called out to them. "No matter what happens, life goes on, and you will have to eat or you will not be strong enough to get through all this."

Reluctantly they sat at the table and tried to eat, but with little success. The dishes remained full, the spoons turned idle. Only the coffee went down.

"My mother used to have a saying," Zia Louisa said sadly. "On every door there is a cross. This is yours." She looked at Rose's swollen belly. "You will have a son," she said. "I just have the feeling." She turned back to Maria and Cesare. "She will have a son, and it will be your grandson. That's how life is. It goes on. You understand what I'm saying? Time will pass and life will get easier."

"You think we forget?" Cesare asked her bitterly.

"No, of course not. These things you don't forget. They stay with you forever. But you learn to live with them. You have to learn. Otherwise you would die yourself from the pain."

And so it was September, and the grapes were purple and heavy, the air still soft and warm, and in the last wave of light the gold star glittered in the front window of the house across the street.

12

It was late October now, and in Columbus Park the trees were ablaze with scarlet and orange and mulberry, the ground a carpet of fallen leaves. In the neighborhood there was the frequent aromatic tang of leaves and twigs burning in trash cans.

Gianna used to love autumn, the smell of it, the sights of it, the flurry of school activities. But now she had lost the love of life. The shadow of her brother's death hung over her like a black cloud shutting out the sunlight.

She saw him everyplace she went, felt his presence in everything she did. His voice, his smile, were branded in her very being, and she ached with the pain.

He was every black-haired soldier she saw walking down the street, every young man with his arm around a girl. Whenever she saw a young couple close together, laughing and whispering, she remembered the last day she and Eddy had sat in the park and he had told her about the girl he loved and wanted to marry after the war. She wished she could talk to her, or even write to her. But she didn't know where she lived, didn't know anything about her except that her name was Teresa.

Some day, Gianna thought, maybe she would tell the family about her. But not now. It would only make things harder for them.

And now she questioned everything she had ever believed in. She looked at the world around her and thought about all the other young men who were dying in the war, day by day, week by week. When she saw an old man, crippled and half blind, sitting sad and alone on a park bench, she would think bitterly, "He is old and sick and has lived out his life. Why is he alive and my brother, who was young and just beginning his life, dead? Why? Why?"

The question tormented her until she knew no peace. There is no God, she thought. It's all a fraud. There's nothing beyond this life either, nothing but the cold fact of death itself, a final ending. There is no afterlife, no beautiful heaven waiting for the faithful, no possibility of someday being reunited with loved ones in a life without tears.

No, it was all a fraud.

She still went to Mass and even to communion sometimes, though hating her hypocrisy. But she couldn't tell her mother and sisters of her feelings. Their faith was what kept them going.

Especially her mother. Gianna marveled that Maria, having lost her son, could go to early Mass and communion every morning. And often she would see her mother sitting on her bed, facing the saint in the glass case on the bureau, and the rosary beads would move through her fingers as she said her Hail Marys.

Gianna wanted to cry out to her, "There is nothing,

Mama, you're praying for nothing! There's no one listening to you!"

And so the days passed, one into another, slowly, painfully, like shadows without substance, without reality. School was a blessing in a way, for in Latin and English and French emotions were not involved, only intellect.

One day Annamarie and Rose said they should give Eddy's clothes to the Salvation Army, and Gianna lashed out at them in anger.

"Don't you give anything of his away! Leave his clothes where they are!"

It seemed to her almost a sacrilege to disturb his things, as if in keeping them intact it was a denial of his death.

"Leave them," Maria said wisely. "Leave them for now."

And often, when the pain was unbearable, Gianna would go into the boys' room to look at Eddy's books and trophies. And wrap her arms around his blue sports jacket and weep.

One day her mother found her there.

"Gianna, sit down here on the bed, and we'll talk a minute."

They sat on one of the beds and her mother took her hand. "Gianna, you have to let go of Eddy."

She stared in disbelief. "Mama, how can you say that?"

"Because you have to let go. You can't go on like this."

"You mean—you've forgotten him?"

"I'm not talking about forgetting. How can you say that?" Maria's eyes clouded with pain. "But there's a difference between remembering and refusing to accept reality."

"Reality?" Gianna stared bitterly at her brother's trophies gleaming in the shadows. "What is reality, Mama?"

"It's accepting what you cannot change."

"I'll never accept his death." She turned to her mother. "How can you go on praying to a God who is never there, who never hears you?"

Maria smiled then. "But He is there, He is always there for me."

"Then you're lucky, Mama. Because He's not there for me. Not any more."

She expected to see shock in her mother's face. Instead she saw sympathy.

"Then I feel sorry for you, my daughter. Because if you don't believe that, what else is there?"

"Nothing, Mama. Nothing."

There was a silence between them, her mother seeming to search for the right words. Then Maria went over to the shelves of books and took down a small Bible. She thumbed through the pages.

"I'm not a Bible reader," she said. "In my day the church never told you to read it. But there is one passage I heard someone tell about once that never left me. It seemed to sum up all of life." Her fingers stopped turning the pages. "Here it is. In Ecclesiastes.

" 'To every thing there is a season, and a time to every purpose under the heaven: A time to be born, and a time to die; . . . a time to weep, and a time to laugh; a time to mourn, and a time to dance. . . .'

"This was written so many, many years ago. And yet it's as true today as it was then. Do you understand what it's saying, Gianna? There's a time for all things. That's what life really is. Life isn't just getting what you want, always being happy, everything being fair and just. There are lots of tears along the way. You're born and you die, you get and you lose."

She took Gianna into her arms, close to the soft warmth of her own body. "I'm not telling you never to cry. Of course you must. What I'm saying is to believe that there is a God who loves you and that you can turn to when it gets too hard. Stop living in the past and think of your own future."

But Gianna murmured, heartbrokenly, "I just can't, Mama. I just can't."

She didn't tell her mother that there were nights when, lying awake in the dark, the ache in her heart was so bad she wished she wouldn't have to wake up in the morning.

She was thinking about Eddy when the big sign crashed down. It happened so quickly she saw only a frightening slant of glass and metal, so close she felt the force of it shuddering past her like a sudden, cold, heavy wind. In the shock of it she reeled back against the window of the five-and-ten cent store.

There was a sudden confusion, people rushing to her side. Cars slowing down, more people hurrying across the street to see what had happened. Voices demanding, solicitous.

"Are you all right?"

"Are you hurt?"

She was numb. "What happened?" she managed to ask.

"You're some lucky girl," a woman said. "That neon sign they were putting up over the jewelers fell down and just grazed by you. Another half inch and you wouldn't be standing here now."

When Gianna saw the heavy sign on the sidewalk, and the splinters of glass, she started to cry.

A man touched her shoulder. "Are you sure you're all right? You didn't get hurt by it at all?"

"I'm fine, I'm fine."

The blind beggar woman sitting in front of Kresge's held out her canvas chair to her. "Sit down," she advised. Another woman handed her a cup of coffee. "Drink this. You'll feel better."

The coffee slid down her throat, warm, familiar. She looked silently at the concerned faces around her. Faces of strangers. She had never seen them before and would probably never see them again.

But for these moments they cared what happened to her.

In the center of downtown New Haven was the Green, two large blocks of grass and elms and diagonal walks. Because it was fairly warm today there was much activity. Old men, thin, shabby, in sweaters and baggy pants, played checkers on the long wooden tables, sunlight flickering through golden elms and glinting on grizzled beards and gray and white heads. They played with great enjoyment, as if realizing that soon the Green would be cold and windy and the tables put away until spring. They would then return to their lives of lonely desolation in rooming houses and hotels and occasional jail cells. For just a little while more they would be able to enjoy this companionship.

Mothers wheeled baby carriages, little boys played ball on the grass, lovers strolled arm in arm.

Gianna sat on a bench and felt the sun warm on her face. She touched one hand with the other, ran her tongue over her lips. She wanted to laugh, to shout with joy to the passersby: "Look, I'm alive! I'm alive! I could have been killed just now, but I'm alive!"

The closeness of her brush with death filled her with awe of the delicate fragility of life itself. Life was like a gossamer thread, she thought, that could be severed and destroyed in a moment. And now she knew how precious life was to her, how much she wanted to live.

Everything she saw right now was beautiful to her. Across the street were the three churches—Center and United, both prim, white, and New Englandish; Trinity, dignified and Anglican—their shadows falling across the lawns and diagonal walks behind them. Up the block loomed the tawny walls of Yale, students flowing in and out of the high iron gates.

Gianna watched an old woman on the next bench feeding bread crumbs to the pigeons. The birds flew all around the woman, one even perched on her foot, as she chatted with them happily.

And on the corner the popcorn vendor was doing a brisk business.

Yes, it was wonderful to be alive on this beautiful golden October day.

Gianna glanced down at her watch. It was getting late. She was already over her lunch hour. Since this was Saturday she was working a full day at the Book Shoppe.

She crossed the street, glad the store was only a half block away. Annamarie was quite strict about her getting back on time.

As she walked past Trinity Church, she heard organ music flowing through the open doors, and almost without realizing it she went up the steps and into the church.

She had never been inside a Protestant church before. That was something a good Catholic just did not do, except for weddings and funerals. But now, sitting in one of the pews, seeing the sunlit shadows streaming down from the brilliant stained windows, the golden cross on the altar, and the shadowy white statues lining the wall behind the altar, it seemed to her that it really wasn't any different from her own church. If there was a God, then He must be here as well.

If there was a God. There was in her a sudden burning hunger to know for sure, to believe, to feel the peace of Christ come into her heart.

Help me, she prayed. If You are real, then come to me now.

And then she knew it wasn't a fraud. Knew it because of the warm, glowing serenity that filled her. Knew it because suddenly the anger and the hate and the bitterness were all gone.

You saved my life just now. Why? Was it just chance, or was there a purpose? Is all this sorrow and pain part of a plan? Is it? If I could only believe that it would make everything so much easier.

Her mother believed it. She always said that God had a purpose for each person's life. Like when Nick made St. Peter's Basilica out of sugar and everyone else marveled at the genius of it. But her mother had not been the least surprised.

"It's God's gift to Nick," she'd said. "God gives every person a special gift, something they have to do with their life. And each person is different. And God knows everything about each person, everything you're doing, everything you're thinking, everything."

Gianna had found this difficult to believe. "But, Mama, there are millions and millions of people on this earth. How can God know everything about every person?"

"He can. He even has every hair on your head numbered, that's how special every person is to Him."

"But that's impossible, Mama. For millions of people?"

"That's why God is God and you are you," was the best explanation her mother could offer.

The organ music filled the sunlit shadows of the church. And Gianna thought of the Bible passage her mother had read to her: "A time to be born and a time to die. A time to mourn and a time to dance."

And she remembered the time she had seen a cardinal in the backyard. Red and beautiful, it had perched for a moment on the peach tree. She had watched it in breathless wonder, hoping it would stay for awhile. But it took wing and she never saw it again.

She thought now that her brother was like that cardinal. He had flashed across the sky of their lives in a fleeting glance of love and beauty, in that golden time when all dreams were possible. But he had never left them, really. He was woven into the tapestry of their lives, a part of them forever.

She returned to work. When she opened the door of the Book Shoppe, Annamarie glanced down at her watch and said, "I was ready to send out a search party for you. What happened? Do you realize you took almost two hours for lunch?"

Gianna laughed and hugged her sister. "Something happened to me today. Something terrible and something wonderful."

That night she wrapped her arms around the blue sports jacket for the last time, and without tears.

I loved you dearly, my brother, and I'll never forget you. But the time has come when I must stop this mourning for you. It is time now for me to begin living my own life again.

13

She made Annamarie promise not to say anything about the sign falling. "Mama would get terribly upset for nothing, and I want to tell Papa about it when I get him alone. I have a special reason."

Her father had withdrawn into a private, silent world of his own. He hardly talked to anyone any more. They all watched him with great love and concern. And helplessness, because they could not seem to reach out to him.

"I try to help him," Maria said often. "But he shuts me out. It's like he has this terrible burden crushing him under and he won't let anyone share it with him."

On Sunday afternoon Gianna found Cesare where she thought he would be, in Waterside Park down near the harbor, about a half mile away. It was here that the men from the neighborhood gathered on Sunday afternoons in warm weather to play *bocci.*

On this late October afternoon the park was empty and desolate looking. The trees were partially bare now, the foliage gold and rust, and the ground was soggy with fallen leaves that had turned brown. From the harbor came a cold, biting wind, a reminder that winter would soon be coming.

Cesare sat on a bench, a lonely figure in the sunlight, staring out at the water.

Gianna sat down beside him and said softly, "Papa—"

He turned quickly, his face a mask of pain and anger. "Why you here? Why you follow me?"

"Papa, I want to talk to you. I know how you feel."

Bitterness filled his face. "What you mean—you know how I feel?"

"You're not alone, Papa. I'm hurting, too. We're all hurting."

He leaned forward and covered his face with his hands.

"Go ahead and cry, Papa, don't be ashamed. You can't hold it in forever, you'll be sick if you try. You have to talk about it, get it out of your system."

Tears trickled slowly through his fingers, down his hands. And then he sighed and took out his handkerchief. He wiped his eyes and blew his nose.

"Don't you feel better now?" she asked him.

He laughed a little. "Maybe I got the wrong one studying to be a doctor."

"Papa, let's talk like we used to."

Cesare lit a cigar and stared out at the water, his face serious again. "What you want to talk about?"

"Eddy."

His face hardened. "No, I don't talk about Eddy. Your mother, she sent you to follow me?"

"No, Papa, she doesn't know anything about it. She doesn't even know where you go when you go out. I came because—I need you, Papa."

"Need me? What you mean, need me?"

"To talk to, Papa."

"You got nobody to talk to? Your mother, your sisters, your girlfriend?"

"I want to talk to you, Papa."

He blew a cloud of smoke, the smell dearly familiar. "So? Talk."

She looked out at the water. It was cold and gray now. The afternoon was quickly darkening. She longed for the sunshine.

"We've lost Eddy, Papa, but we can't change anything. We have to remember all the happy things about him. The way he laughed at life, the nice things he said and did."

"You think I don't remember?"

"But you remember him only in grief, Papa. Eddy wouldn't want us to keep crying for him. You know that."

"But he's gone. Forever. When the war's over, the other boys, they come home again. But not my son. He's never come back. As long as I live, Eddy's never come back."

"There's something else you should think of, Papa. What it says in the Bible."

"What?"

"Jesus said that we would all be together again some day, that it would be a life without tears. We have to believe that, Papa, believe that this life on earth as we know it is not all there is, just a small part."

"You believe that?" His black eyes were burning through her.

She searched for the right words. "Yes, Papa, I believe it. I believe that life never dies. That what we have here is just a small part of our existence, and that when we die it's like closing a door on one room and stepping into another.

"Papa, I had something very strange and wonderful happen to me yesterday. I was walking along the street feeling bitter and depressed, as I have been since Eddy died, and thinking how I hated life and nothing in it had any meaning for me any more. I'd even given up believing in God, if you want the truth.

"And suddenly this heavy neon sign fell—a man was installing it over a store—Papa, it missed me by maybe half an inch. I actually felt it go by me."

Cesare turned pale. His hands trembled. "Why you don't say something about it last night?"

"Because I wanted to tell you about it when we were alone. It was something strange, Papa. When I realized how close I came to getting killed I suddenly knew how precious and beautiful my life was to me. That in spite of all the sorrow and pain I was glad to be alive. And there was something else I thought about, Papa."

"What?"

"It made me wonder about the purpose of life, why some young people die and yet so many old, sick people go on living. I asked myself if maybe God does have a special purpose for each person's life.

"I mean—maybe Eddy had done whatever it was that God had put him on earth to do. And maybe—maybe it wasn't my time yet. Maybe God's got something special He wants me to do with my life."

Her father had been listening intently to her. He smiled a little now. "So, Gianna mia, what you do now? Become a nun?"

She laughed. "No, Papa, believe me, I'm not cut out to be a nun. But I'll tell you something. That changed my whole way of thinking. I feel—oh, I can't tell you how wonderful I feel. Like I never really believed in God before. Like—suddenly I was starting a whole new life. It seemed to me God was saying, 'Look, stop all this hurting, just tell it to Me and I'll make it easier.' I didn't feel the anger and the bitterness any more.

"Suddenly I have all these marvelous things I want to do. And you, too, Papa, you can start a new life."

He eyed her with suspicion. "What you want me to do?"

She put her hand over his, gripped it tightly. "Stop grieving over Eddy."

"You mean—forget him?" he asked, incredulously.

"No, of course not. We'll never forget him or stop loving him. But stop grieving. We can't change what's happened, nothing can ever bring him back. But we can stop living in the past.

"I thought of something yesterday. Remember that time I told you I saw the red bird in the yard—the cardinal? It was so beautiful and I wished it would stay longer. But then it flew away and I didn't see it again. Remember? Well, I got to thinking that Eddy was like that cardinal. You know what I mean? We had him for only a short time, but that time was full of love and beauty. We should be grateful for that time.

"And there are so many other good things to live for, Papa. You have Mama and the rest of us. And, Papa, you have a grandchild waiting to be born."

Her father sighed, reluctant to let go of the past, yet part of him longing for the future. "And if it's a boy—" he began wryly.

"And if it's a boy," Gianna laughed, "he'll be named for you! Rose said she would stick your name in there somewhere."

They talked a little longer, of other things, her school work, her bond selling at the movie theater. And then the afternoon became dark and the wind colder. Cesare stood up.

"Come, we go home now. Your mother, she'll be worried."

As they came to St. Michael's, Gianna had a sudden impulse. "Papa, let's go in and light a candle. For Eddy."

Cesare shook his head. "No, I don't go. You go if you want. I wait out here."

She went alone into the solemn stillness of the church and hurried up the side aisle to the table of votive candles. They flickered serenely in their tiny red glass holders.

She hesitated for a moment, her head bowed. God, God, help my father to believe the way You helped me.

Then, as she reached for the long taper, a man's large, calloused hand also reached, and she turned to see Cesare looking down at her with misty eyes.

"I light it," he said softly, dropping a coin into the box. "And we say the prayer together. For Eddy."

She said an extra prayer, thanking God for bringing her father into the church, and when she glanced up at Cesare he was still praying. After a moment he stood up and touched her arm. "Come, we go home now."

Outside, in the unlit darkness, Gianna said, "Mama used to say when we were small that no matter what happened in life, no matter how bad it was, if you had your faith and your family, you could endure anything. It's true, you know, Papa."

He smiled in the darkness. "Your mother, she's a smart woman. She's always right. Only don't tell her I said so."

"Papa—"

"Yes, Gianna mia?"

"Papa, Mama needs you. She's hurting, too. You need each other, you could help each other."

He sighed. "I know, I know. Well, from now on maybe things will get better for all of us."

When they opened the kitchen door there was the welcoming smell of veal chops baking in the oven with potatoes and peas. Maria was at the kitchen table reading the Sunday paper. She looked worried.

"Where've you been?" she demanded. "I've been worried sick." She looked astonished when Cesare laughed and kissed her on the cheek.

"You've been drinking?" she asked suspiciously. "With Gianna?"

They all laughed, and the laughter was a beautiful

thing, rich and tender, and full of love.

Maria remembered then. "Oh, and the most important thing of all I'm forgetting to tell you. Rose went to the hospital this afternoon. She's in labor."

When the telephone rang, Maria dropped her crocheting and rushed to answer it. Happiness spread over her face. She turned to Cesare and the girls, tears shining in her eyes.

"It's Mario," she said. "Rose just had a baby boy. Cesare, Mario wants to talk to you. He has a special message from Rose."

Cesare took the phone. Gianna watched her father's face as pain and pleasure intermingled in it, and then the pleasure took over and he was all smiles.

"And my grandson, he's already got a name," he announced proudly to the family. "My grandson, he's named Edward Cesare!"

Rose had kept her promise.

14

The snow was coming down heavily. In the streets the cars and buses were turning it into slush, but on the sidewalks it still lay white and soft and lovely.

Gianna hurried along in the crowd, her head bent against the cold wind, her school books held tightly to her. In three weeks it would be Christmas. Everywhere she went there were the gaudy, brilliant symbols of it. The stores glittered with tinseled trees and lights and decorations, and Santa Claus was ubiquitous, in every department store, on street corners, even in the five-and-ten. Gianna heard one wary boy ask his mother how Santa could be in so many places at the same time, and the mother, perplexed for an answer, replied, "Santa Claus is something like God. He can be everywhere at the same time."

The stores were crowded with masses of shoppers and women with crying children, and both clerks and customers were reaching the point of weary impatience and short-fused tempers. Christmas did seem to bring out the worst in people, Gianna thought.

And yet there was, overall, a frenzied gaiety, a reaching out for happiness, as if in celebrating Christmas they could forget some of the heartbreak of the war.

There was a reminder, too, that Christmas was more than cards and gifts and Santa Claus. In front of Kresge's, a Salvation Army woman, in black cape and bonnet, kept watch over the big iron kettle, her face and hands red with cold, and the ringing of her bell sounded warm and merry in the frosty afternoon air.

Gianna remembered another Christmas five years ago, when life had seemed so blissfully perfect. She remembered meeting Eddy on the street Christmas Eve, and how big and handsome he'd looked under the street light, snowflakes in his hair, a bag of Christmas presents in his hand. And then later, all of them gathered in the living room, trimming the tree, and Nonna still alive, smiling and serene in the midst of her family.

Gianna thought, All my life Christmas was the most exciting time of the year. But this year is different.

It was different. It was hardly spoken of at home. For the first time in her life there would be no Christmas tree, no mistletoe, no elaborate baking. It was as if they were all denying the fact of Christmas, wishing it away.

They had learned to live with the reality of Eddy's death. The bitter grief had given way to resignation and acceptance. But now, with the coming of the holidays, the sadness had returned.

Cesare had become quiet and withdrawn again, and Maria seemed to spend more time sitting with her rosary beads in her fingers, looking out at the street with sorrowful eyes as if remembering all the times she had seen her son hurry up that street.

Gianna and Annamarie were always saying to each

other, "I wish Christmas was over. I hate the holidays now."

Only Rose's life seemed pleasant and serene. In her new role of motherhood, in the daily joys of tending to her baby and home and husband, she was unable to let grief take over her life. And so she had a different perspective.

"You have to make life as bright and cheerful for Mama and Papa as you can," she would tell her younger sisters. "Try to keep them from thinking too much. Don't let the house be too quiet when you're home."

Rose did as much as she could. Every day she either brought the baby over to see Maria or made Maria come down to her house for a cup of coffee. She still lived in her mother-in-law's house down the street, as she and Mario had decided to wait until after the war to buy a house.

Gianna walked through the Green, even though it was windier there. She liked the open air, liked feeling the snow cold and tingly on her face.

She was anxious to get to work this afternoon, for this was the day Christopher Branning was coming to work part time at the Book Shoppe.

He was a divinity student at Yale, and after his ordination in June he would go to South America as a missionary. The owner of the Book Shoppe said that Christopher had spent his early boyhood in China, where his parents were missionaries. They were executed by the Communists when they refused to leave the country, and the boy's life was saved by Chinese converts who smuggled him out of China. He'd spent the rest of his growing-up years with a minister and his wife who had been friends of his parents.

Gianna was looking forward to meeting him. She thought he sounded fascinating.

When she reached the Book Shoppe she stood for a moment in the falling snow and looked at the window she had decorated with such loving care. She had to admire the beauty of it.

On a bed of rich red velvet rested a copy of Dickens' *Christmas Carol,* its open pages marked by a very old leather bookmark. A fat red electric candle burned in a wrought iron holder. It was so simple, a refreshing change from the gaudy displays that cluttered so many of the store windows downtown. It seemed especially fitting for this shop, blending in with the early New England style of the small-paned windows and the polished brass knocker gleaming on the white door.

When Annamarie first saw it from the outside, she had remarked, "I swear, Gianna, I almost expect to step inside and see women in big bonnets and long dresses with bustles."

Now, looking into the shop itself, Gianna saw a tall, thin young man with blond hair standing beside Annamarie, and the two of them were laughing about something.

The bell tinkled when she opened the door, and Annamarie said, "Gianna, this is Chris Branning. Chris, this is my sister."

The first thing Gianna really noticed about him was the blueness of his eyes.

"Well, this is the archaeologist," he said, and his smile was warm and gentle.

Gianna grinned at her sister. "I see you've been talking about me."

"Yes, we have," Christopher said, his blue eyes twinkling. "I understand you want to go searching for lost civilizations."

"That's right."

"Well, now I can add that to my list of firsts. You're the first girl I ever met who wanted to be an archaeologist. I think that's great."

She took off her coat. "I should have you talk to my father. He thinks it's all a little crazy. Most people do."

She had felt his amusement, but he was quite serious when he said, "Well, different people have different dreams. We each have to follow our own path."

For a moment she looked into Christopher Branning's eyes and had a startled remembrance of Eddy once saying something like that. He understands, she thought; he has dreams of his own.

As the afternoon passed she often found herself glancing over at him, watching him as he moved around the bookshelves and waited on customers. She thought of him as a boy, crouched in hiding as his parents were killed before his eyes. She looked forward to long talks with him when the bustle of Christmas was over. There were so many questions to ask. She wanted to know about the mission he was going to, what he wanted to do down there. For the first time she had met a young man other than her own brothers who was intellectually challenging.

During the afternoon Mrs. Donato hurried into the shop, flushed and puffing. She was bubbling over with excitement. "Annamarie, did you get Sal's letter yet?"

"Which one?"

"The important one! He got a pass for Christmas!"

Annamarie's eyes lit up. "Did he? How marvelous!"

Mrs. Donato's face clouded slightly. "It is and it isn't. I have the feeling that he'll be shipping out after this leave." But then she smiled. "He says he has a surprise for me. I'll bet you know what it is."

"A surprise?"

Sal's mother squeezed Annamarie's arm and smiled knowingly at Gianna. "Oh, that's all right. He wants to surprise me. I won't try to get it out of you, but I'm sure I know what it is. Well, I'll see you Christmas, anyway, when Sal's home. So long now, girls."

When she left, Annamarie stood at the window and stared out at the falling snow. She seemed far away in her thoughts.

Gianna asked, "What surprise is that?"

Annamarie turned to her with a smile. "I guess he means getting engaged. That's all he writes about these days." She laughed lightly and met Christopher's eyes across the room. "Who knows? Maybe he is the knight on a white horse after all. Maybe I've been too slow to recognize him."

"Well, don't get high-pressured into anything," Gianna warned her.

A cold wind swept across Columbus Park. The wooden benches rattled in its wake, and the trees, still lightly crusted with snow, shivered and bent against the sunless December sky.

As Maria and the girls walked to church, a man's voice called out to them, and they turned to see Sal Donato hurrying to catch up with them.

Annamarie's face brightened. "Sal! I thought you wouldn't get home until tomorrow."

"I was lucky. I got a ride on one of the military planes. Hi, Mrs. Dellesanto, Gianna."

Gianna greeted him warmly, and Maria gave him a hug. "You look real good, Sal. Welcome home."

But Sal couldn't take his eyes off Annamarie. "It sure is good to be here," he said, slipping his arm through hers.

Maria pulled Gianna forward. "Let them walk alone," she murmured. "They have things to talk about. They don't need us."

During Mass Gianna frequently glanced sideways at her sister and Sal. Annamarie looked radiant. Her dark eyes were shining, and there was a glowing happiness in her face. And she didn't pull her hand away when Sal reached out for it and held it.

Maybe she does love him, Gianna thought. Maybe she just had to see him to be sure. Still, getting engaged to him, being committed, that was something else. The war could last a long time yet. Maybe she wouldn't see him for a couple of years. Would she still care about him when he returned?

Suppose he got wounded, suppose he never came back. Like Eddy.

Gianna was glad she was just a high-school senior.

Her life seemed so much simpler. She didn't have to worry about falling in love or getting engaged and having someone go off to war. She hadn't even started to go out with boys yet. Aside from the fact that Cesare had never allowed his daughters to date while still in high school, she was too busy studying and working. Boys were fine to argue with in school, or work with on the school paper. But that was it. They all seemed so young and immature. She felt more like a big sister to them. That was why she found Christopher Branning so interesting. At least she could talk to him.

Even Dominique was going steady, with a Marine she had met at a USO dance. Gianna thought she was foolish. Here she was still in high school and tying herself down already. On the other hand, knowing Dominique's flightiness and her mother's domination, it was unlikely the romance would last too long anyway.

Gianna's thoughts turned to Muriel. She hadn't seen her for three years, not since her mother remarried and they moved to California. But Muriel wrote to Gianna and Dominique, and they all agreed that one day when the war was over they would get together again.

After Mass Maria invited Sal to dinner and he accepted laughingly, his hand still holding Annamarie's. "You didn't think I was really going home right now, did you?"

He and Annamarie walked close together down the church steps and out into the cold gloominess of the December morning. On the sidewalk Zia Louisa smiled at them and murmured something to Maria.

"Now we see," she said, wagging a finger at Annamarie.

At home Cesare was having wine with Leonardo at the kitchen table. He stood up and grasped Sal's hand. "Sal! Welcome home."

Sal said, "Hello, Mr. Dellesanto." He turned to his grandfather. "Hi, Nonno. Didn't know you were here."

Cesare beamed paternally at him. "Every Sunday, Sal! Well, this is like family reunion. We're all one big family, right? Sit down, sit down. Annamarie, get Sal some coffee. You want wine, Sal?"

"No, thanks, just coffee."

"It's A-1 stuff. I made it myself."

"No, thanks, the coffee will be fine."

Sal stayed for Sunday dinner, and Rose and Mario came with the baby, as they always did. After dinner Rose asked, "Who wants to give the baby his bottle?"

Annamarie held out her arms. "Here, give him to me."

Everyone laughed and watched as Annamarie cradled little Eddy in her arms. Sal sat close beside her on the sofa, his eyes never leaving her.

Rose sighed. "I love Sunday," she said. "I can get to feel like a lady of leisure again."

"When were you ever a lady of leisure?" Gianna asked wryly.

When the baby finished the bottle, Rose started to take him from Annamarie, but Maria motioned her away.

"What's the hurry?" she asked. "The baby's happy where he is."

"Can't say that I blame him," Sal remarked.

And Gianna had to smile at the shrewd workings of her mother's mind. It was obvious that Maria wanted Sal to see how good Annamarie was with babies. Although from the looks of things that didn't seem to be necessary.

Later Annamarie and Sal left to go to Sal's house for awhile, and Rose and Mario went home with the baby.

That afternoon Cesare and Leonardo sat at the kitchen table with a bottle of wine between them and talked in low voices, laughing often. Gianna and Maria were in the living room, Gianna studying her Latin, Maria crocheting a doily for a niece's bridal shower.

"Those two act as if they have a gloriously happy secret between them," Gianna said, glancing up from her book.

Her mother smiled. "Don't you know why?"

"You mean—Annamarie and Sal?"

"Of course."

Gianna laughed. "You mean, like two family dynasties being united?"

"Oh, don't be funny. I can tell you something. Once those two are engaged it will be all over the neighborhood the same day. Your father and Leonardo will celebrate for a week."

"They sound as if they've already started."

Maria listened to the men's voices in the kitchen. "Papa needs something to be happy about. He's been feeling low lately."

"It's Christmas. We all feel it. But I guess it would be nice if Annamarie and Sal did get engaged."

Her mother looked curiously at her. "You don't think so?"

"I said I thought it would be nice."

"But you don't sound too enthusiastic."

"Well, to tell you the truth, Mama, Annamarie hasn't said that much about him. As close as we are, she never once said she was in love with him."

"So—she has to tell you to make it official?"

"No, but it seems she would have said it by now."

"Well, take it from a mother, those two will be engaged. Today. You'll see. I saw that look in Sal's eyes."

The three of them were in the living room listening to the news on the radio when Annamarie and Sal returned. There was no doubt as to what had happened. They were both starry eyed and laughing.

Annamarie held out her hand with the new diamond solitaire sparkling on it. "Look, everybody," she said gaily. "We're engaged!"

Her mother and sister admired her ring and embraced her and Sal, and Cesare kept pumping Sal's hand and repeating, "Welcome to the family!"

Maria said laughingly, a catch in her voice, "Now I'll have to finish that bedspread."

Annamarie hugged her. "Don't hurry, Mama, the wedding won't be for quite awhile."

And Gianna thought, Maybe it will be a happy Christmas after all.

15

On the morning of Christmas Eve Gianna came downstairs for breakfast to find her mother red eyed and pensive.

"Morning, Mama. What's the matter? You've been crying?"

Maria turned away. She brushed at the tears welling in her eyes and busied herself with Gianna's fried egg and toast. "Don't ask," she said. "It's just a passing mood."

Gianna sighed. "I know how you feel, Mama. It's even harder when it's a holiday. No matter how you try to be cheerful, deep down the hurt is there. Maybe —maybe it will be better next Christmas."

Her mother looked at her with sorrowing eyes. "How can it be better? Will he ever be back?" She placed Gianna's breakfast on the table.

"Have a cup of coffee with me, Mama. Just the two of us."

Maria poured herself some coffee and sat down. "There's something else," she said.

"Oh? What's that, Mama?"

"Your brother."

"Paolo?"

"Yes, Paolo. Something's not right with him. Didn't you notice? Since he came home for Christmas he has been very quiet."

"Maybe he's thinking about Eddy, too."

"No, it's something else. I have the feeling—I have the feeling he's changing his mind about being a priest."

Gianna remembered how Paolo had been acting since he came home a few days ago. Quiet, secretive. Always going somewhere, and angry when anyone asked where. His reluctance to talk about the seminary.

"They all go through periods of doubt, Mama. Maybe that's what it is with him now. Maybe he's uncertain."

Maria's eyes burned. "He was born to be a priest. You know it as well as I do."

"No, I don't know it, Mama. And you don't either. Only he can decide. Besides, what's so terrible if he changes his mind?"

Her mother glared angrily at her. "That would be the worst thing he could do."

"Mama, let him make up his own mind." Gianna patted her mother's hand across the table and swallowed the last of her coffee. "Well, I haven't time to solve the problems of the whole Dellesanto family right now. I have to go to work. I promised Annamarie I'd get to the shop earlier this morning. It will be a busy day with people doing last-minute shopping."

Before she left the house Gianna gave her mother a hug. "Be brave, Mama, the way you always are. Just keep your mind on happy thoughts. Like Annamarie getting engaged, and Rose's baby, and Julio and Valerie coming today. Let's make it as good a Christmas as we can. Promise?"

Her mother smiled wanly. "Don't worry. I'll be all right. By this afternoon I'll be A-1, as your father would say."

It was time to close up for the holiday. Annamarie and Sal were checking a light in the back of the shop while Christopher helped Gianna into her coat.

The shop looked so empty and still, with only the night lights on. Gianna looked at Christopher and said, "Why don't you come home with us, Chris? The invitation's still open."

He squeezed her shoulder and smiled down at her. "I really appreciate your concern for me, both you and Annamarie. And I would really like to come. But I already promised to have dinner with a few of my friends at school. They can't get home for the holidays. Some of them are from halfway around the world, you know. And then I'll be having the Christmas Eve service at my church."

He conducted services for a tiny Episcopal church in a town just outside of New Haven, whose congregation was too small for a full-time minister.

Sal had his father's car and offered to drive Christopher back to school, but he refused, saying he liked to walk.

Gianna turned and looked after him as he hurried down the dark street, his collar turned up against the wind. Her heart went out to him. She wanted to run after him, walk beside him in the cold night. She had the sudden longing to spend Christmas Eve with him, wondering what it would be like to have dinner with him in the great dining hall at school, to meet those unknown friends of his who came from halfway around the world, and later to sit in the candlelit glow of the little country church and listen to him preach.

She wondered what Annamarie would say if she knew how much she liked Christopher, how much she thought of him when she was away from the shop. She felt so close to him. For the first time since Eddy died there was someone who could really understand what she wanted to do with her life.

"He must have such a lonely Christmas," she mused.

"Well, we did invite him home with us," Annamarie reminded her. "Remember? Besides, what's so lonely about him? He's going to be with his close friends and his parishioners."

"But they're not family."

Annamarie was staring at her. "Well, we're not either."

"He doesn't have anyone in the world that he's related to. Even the people who raised him died a long time ago."

"Gianna, you're being melodramatic. I think you should be a writer instead of an archaeologist. Chris is quite happy, believe me. You're giving him a sadness he just doesn't have."

You don't know him, Gianna thought. You don't know him as well as I do.

She had dreaded going home on Christmas Eve, expecting her parents to be in low spirits, expecting even the house to have sad memories of its own. But when she opened the kitchen door there was brightness and gaiety, and the rich smells of the wonderful supper her mother was cooking.

On the back of the stove simmered a big pot of tomato sauce, crab legs pinkly tipping the surface. The last of the shrimp were frying to golden perfection, and Maria was just putting a large pan of fried smelts and the rest of the cooked shrimp into the oven to keep warm. Rose was setting the long kitchen table with a flowered tablecloth and the best dishes, and the flatware she and Mario had given Maria for Christmas. Cesare was having a glass of wine.

"Merry Christmas!" everyone called out to the new arrivals. Julio and Valerie came in from the living room. "Well, it looks like I'm going to lose another sister," Julio said.

Annamarie poked him in the ribs. "What do you mean—lose a sister? Where am I going?"

"He means you're joining the ranks of committed women," Valerie said.

"Let's have a toast before dinner," Julio proposed. "I brought us a delicious Chablis. Everybody go in the living room."

Maria protested. "I'm cooking."

"You're through for the minute," he said, propelling her away from the stove. "Everything's cooked but the macaroni, right? Get out of the kitchen for a few minutes. Valerie, go call Paolo. I think he's upstairs."

When they were all gathered, Julio passed out the glasses of white wine. "To the spirit of Christmas," he said, his thin dark face serious now. "To what Christmas really means—the birth of love and joy."

They raised their glasses to each other, and for a moment there was the shadow of sadness as they remembered the one who was missing. His picture looked down at them from the mantelpiece.

Gianna felt a lump in her throat. Sometimes, like now, it seemed to her that Eddy had just gone away on a trip and one day they would open the door and he would be there waiting, warm and alive. And the girl named Teresa would be with him, and he would say, Look, everyone, this is the girl I'm going to marry.

Stop it, stop it, she told herself sharply. He is dead, he is never going to walk into this house again. You will never see him again in this lifetime.

She saw her father squeeze her mother's shoulder, silently.

Then the baby began to cry and the moment of sadness passed. Maria grabbed little Eddy from the carriage and rocked him violently in her arms. *"Bello, bello,"* she crooned soothingly, and the crying ceased.

"See?" Rose said. "Mama still has the knack, even after all these years."

And Cesare chided, "So what you think, a mother

stops being a mother when her children grow up?"

Maria handed the baby over to Annamarie. "Here, you hold him. His bottle's ready. His mother is helping me. And you, too, Gianna, I need you."

"How about me, Mom?" Valerie asked.

Maria hugged her. "Yes, you, too."

"Now you can throw the macaroni," Cesare said.

At the end of the dinner Julio reached over and took his wife's hand. "Shall we tell them the news now?"

"News? What news?" Maria demanded. But she saw their glowing faces and knew. "When?" she asked. "When a son or daughter says they have news it means only one thing."

"Six months," Julio said proudly. He turned to his father. "We want a boy, right, Papa? We have to get that idea across to Valerie. She's partial to girls."

"Girls!" Cesare looked at her. "A grandson you have to give me."

Rose said, "I already gave you a grandson, Papa."

"But your son, he don't carry the family name. I want a Dellesanto grandson. Cesare Dellesanto he can be named."

When the dishes were done and the kitchen straightened up, they all gathered again in the living room and began to open the gifts.

Gianna looked around at her family with love and pride. Instead of the sadness and tears she had expected, there was pleasure in her parents' faces when they smiled at Annamarie and Sal. She saw her tiny nephew sleeping in his carriage in a corner, and remembered the other baby now waiting to be born.

Yes, she thought, there is a time for all things, each thing in its place.

She also saw her brother, Paolo, sitting apart from the others, almost in the shadows of the room, and he looked dark and brooding. He had always been serious and withdrawn, but her mother was right. Now there was something bothering him.

When the gifts had all been opened, Paolo stood up and said, "I'm going out for awhile. I'll see you all later."

Maria watched him as he slipped into his black coat. "Where are you going that's so important you have to leave your family on Christmas Eve?"

But Cesare said, "You got someplace to go, you go. Don't mind your mother. Sometimes she thinks you are still a baby."

After Midnight Mass the people spilled out of the church and onto the sidewalk, where they stood in close, laughing groups. No one seemed to notice the bitter cold or care about the blacked-out darkness.

Zia Louisa called out, "Merry Christmas!" and asked to see Annamarie's ring. She squeezed Sal's arm. "You got a wonderful girl," she said. "The best."

Sal's eyes glowed. "I know."

Dominique and her mother came down the steps and hurried over to exchange holiday greetings and congratulate the happy couple.

Dominique said to Gianna, "I got a card from Muriel. Did you?"

"Yes. She says she's going to visit us one of these days. Wouldn't that be nice? Gee, it's been years since we saw her."

"Who's Muriel?" Julio asked.

"She's a girl who used to live in Dominique's house."

She didn't tell him that Muriel Martin had been her first contact with the outside world. She thought dreamily of those Sunday afternoons when she and Dominique would go to the Martins' flat and Muriel would show them her scrapbooks and souvenirs. Through her they had known Radio City Music Hall and Toffenetti's and other glamorous places they had never dreamed existed.

"Well, we have to go," Dominique said. "Listen, Gianna, come over when you can, okay? Oh, look, it's snowing! We'll have a white Christmas after all."

"I'll try to see you a little while tomorrow maybe. Only a few minutes though."

"All right. If you can't, don't worry about it. I know you have your family home. See you. Merry Christmas, everybody!"

"Well, what are we waiting for?" Cesare demanded impatiently. He had been persuaded by his family to go to church, but he didn't intend to make a night of it.

And then Julio asked, "Hey, isn't that our brother Paolo over there with a girl?"

They all looked. No one said anything. They just gaped.

The girl was small and very pretty in a quiet, delicate way. She wore a black lace mantilla over her long brown hair, and it gave her an air of glamour and mystery. But there was no mystery in the way she smiled at Paolo.

And Paolo—Paolo was no longer the quiet, brooding young man his family knew. With his arm tightly around the girl's shoulders, the snow glimmering on his dark hair, he was laughing and happy.

Together Paolo and the girl walked away from the crowd of people into the bright, snowy night, aware of no one but each other.

"She looks familiar," Julio said. "Who is she?"

His mother answered in a voice of sorrow, "It's Laura Riccitelli."

16

Christopher had brought a new dimension into their lives. In his gentle, quiet way he shared his life with Gianna and Annamarie.

He was so different from any of the men they had known. In a way he was like Paolo, completely disinterested in material things, aesthetic in his mode of living and his cultural tastes. But unlike Paolo he was not moody or introverted. He was very much involved with other people's lives, particularly in his part-time church work and his activities with the underprivileged boys' group at the Y.

Once, in the beginning, Gianna asked him when he had decided to become a minister.

"When I was a small boy in China," he said. "I never wanted to be anything else."

"I'm surprised you didn't change your mind," Gianna said.

"You mean because of my parents?"

"Yes."

"Maybe that made me want to even more. You see, I knew what my parents had accomplished in their mission, how many people they brought to Christ. In fact, it was because of their teachings that my own life was saved. The Chinese converts smuggled me from village to village until I reached the Red Cross. If they had been found out—and maybe some of them were —they would have been tortured or executed."

Gianna sighed. "Chris, you could write a novel about your own life."

Chris's personal tastes were mostly classical, and gradually he interested the girls in reading Tolstoy and Dostoevsky.

"Ever read *War and Peace?"* he asked Gianna one day when they were having a coffee break in the shop.

She shook her head. "No. I read *Anna Karenina,* but when I saw the size of *War and Peace* I just couldn't bring myself to start it."

"You have to read it," he said. "You'd love it. I know you would."

The next day he brought her his own copy, old and battered looking. "It was a gift to me many years ago," he explained. "I'd like you to read it."

She stared at the hugeness of it. "How do you think I'd ever have enough time with all the homework I have?"

"There's no rush. Just read a chapter at a time. Once you get into it you'll be surprised how fast it will go. This book has everything of life in it. Birth and death, war and peace, love and hate. It covers just about every human emotion and circumstance. It's the greatest novel ever written."

"How long did it take you to read it?"

"About a month, I guess."

"It will take me a year."

"Try it. Read it for a week and then tell me you can't or won't finish it."

Annamarie read *Crime and Punishment* and began to go to the library on her lunch hours and listen to Chopin and Rachmaninoff records. At home she would tune in classical music on her little radio in the bedroom.

"He sure is making us intellectuals," Gianna said.

"He sure is," Annamarie agreed. "Before he came into our lives I didn't know Chopin from Beethoven."

"You know, I may be an A student ready for college, but the things he's involved us in I would never have thought I'd care that much for. I mean, who would ever think Tolstoy and Dostoevsky would be that interesting? And yet when you talk to him about these books he makes you feel as if you can actually taste the snow and feel the wind. Julio's a doctor and I never heard him talk about Tolstoy."

"Paolo likes classical things."

"But he never talked to me about them."

Gianna became so starry-eyed when she talked about Christopher in the privacy of the bedroom at night that sometimes her sister would become sharp with her.

"Gianna, you're getting too fond of him. He's a lot older than you. You're only a child to him."

"He's not that old. I'm seventeen and he's twenty-six. Nine years' difference."

"Well, don't get too carried away. It's very easy for a girl your age to get a crush on someone like Christopher. Besides, he's going away in a few months and you'll never see him again after that."

Annamarie was very edgy these days. Everyone at home noticed it.

"She's always flying off the handle," Gianna mentioned once to her mother.

Maria said, "Be patient with your sister. It's not easy being engaged to a man who's away at war, not knowing when he's coming back or if he's coming back."

But Gianna wasn't sure that was the reason. Annamarie didn't even mention Sal much any more, and although she still wrote to him as often as before, her letters seemed to be getting shorter.

Christopher had asked the girls if they would like to come to the divinity school for dinner.

"I don't know, Gianna," Annamarie said later, when the sisters were alone. "You know how Mama and Papa are. Now that I'm engaged they'd consider it the same as going on a date with another man."

"We'll say he invited me and you're just going along."

Annamarie laughed. "That would be worse. Papa won't even let you go out with boys. All you have to say is that you're interested in someone who's going off to be a missionary. And someone who's twenty-six besides."

"Well, you're twenty-one. You don't need permission to go anywhere."

"You know, you have a point there. I'm so used to doing what Mama and Papa want that I forget I don't need their permission." She stared thoughtfully at Gianna. "You really want to go, don't you?"

And Gianna stared back at her. "Don't you?"

"Yes. You know why?"

"Why?"

"We never heard him play the piano."

"He plays the piano?"

"Didn't you know?"

"I never heard him mention it."

"That's because you're not a Chopin fan the way I am."

Annamarie was laughing hard now, and Gianna threw a pillow at her. And then Gianna became suddenly serious. "You know, I just realized something."

"What?"

"That you and I have only a short time to be together like this. I mean—all these years we've shared this room, and laughed in it, and cried in it, and pretty soon it will end."

"What do you mean—end?"

"You know. I'll go away to college, and when Sal comes home you'll be getting married—"

"Gianna Dellesanto, you are such a one for always looking into the future. Never mind what's going to happen six months or a year from now. Just enjoy today, will you?"

"Oh, look who's talking. The hedonist."

"What's a hedonist?"

"Boy, some cultured sister I have. She talks about Chopin and Dostoevsky like she knew them personally. And she doesn't even know what a hedonist is. It's a pleasure lover."

Annamarie reflected for a moment. "Well, I like pleasure."

Gianna threw another pillow at her.

Christopher was delighted when they accepted his invitation. "How about tomorrow?" he suggested.

Maria was quite upset with Annamarie. "You're engaged to be married. An engaged girl doesn't go out with another man when her boyfriend is risking his life overseas. What kind of girl are you?"

"Oh, Mama, this is not going out with another man."

"What is it then?"

"Christopher simply asked Gianna and me to have dinner at his school, in a huge dining hall full of other people. He's going to show us what a divinity school is like."

"So that's a big important thing to you, that you have to see what a divinity school looks like? What's that to you? You're not going to be a minister."

"Oh, Mama."

"No matter how you look at it, it's a date. It's you he's interested in, not Gianna."

Gianna tried to lighten the conversation, which was becoming a little too tense. "Why not me, Mama? Don't you think he could like me? I'm not exactly a child any more. I'm going away to college pretty soon."

Her mother didn't even consider the possibility.

"This is no laughing matter. Don't make jokes."

"Besides," Annamarie said, quietly now, "Christopher Branning is going away in June. To South America. And he's not looking to get tied up with a Catholic girl. That's the very last thing he needs."

Maria stared hard at her. "I can't stop you. You're twenty-one, but you will regret this dinner. I just have the feeling in my bones. Call it a mother's intuition."

Annamarie looked away from her probing eyes. "He's going away in a few months," she said. "We'll never see him again. What difference does it make if we go this one time?"

Her father was studying her now. "Sal's over in the war, giving up everything. He could be getting killed or hurt. Just remember."

"I know, Papa, I know." Gianna thought she caught a note of despair in her sister's voice.

After supper Annamarie started to wash her hair at the kitchen sink. Maria looked up from the table where she was hemming a skirt. "You're washing your hair?"

"What's wrong with that? I had to wash it anyway."

"I see you have your nail polish out, too. My, this is some fancy date tomorrow night, for all you say about it."

"Mama, it's not a date. And stop making something out of nothing. You know very well I always wash my hair and do my nails on Friday night. What's so unusual about that?"

"You also have your coral dress out," her mother observed.

"Well, I have to look presentable, don't I?"

"You have to wear your best dress to look presentable?"

"What do you want me to wear, Mama, my old clothes? Gianna's getting dressed up."

"Gianna's different."

"Why?"

"She's not two-timing the man she's engaged to."

That night Gianna lay awake in the darkness, hugging her fantasies to her. Christopher was on her mind a lot these days. She liked to think he cared about her. How much or in what way she couldn't be sure. But he had shown so much interest in her it had to be something more than friendship.

In fact, they'd had many conversations that did not include Annamarie. Sometimes when Gianna was returning from lunch hour on Saturday afternoons she would come across him sitting on a bench on the upper part of the Green, and she would sit with him for a few minutes and discuss *War and Peace.*

When she talked about him to Dominique, her friend was skeptical. "He's twenty-six. To him you're like a kid sister."

"Then why does he spend so much time sharing things with me?"

"I dunno. Maybe it's just his missionary instincts."

She had one particular fantasy about him. Before he went away he would go to her father and say, "Mr. Dellesanto, I know I'm a stranger to you but I'm in love with your daughter Gianna. I want to marry her and take her away with me to South America."

Of course her father would be furious and throw him out of the house. And of course she would have to turn him down anyway. She had her own career to think of first. She had to go to college—and it might be for six years. But she would never forget him. He had to know that. She would always remember him.

Looking into the brilliantly lighted room of paneled walls and snowy white tablecloths, Gianna saw a sea of men. Most in their twenties, some in their thirties and forties, a few even older. Here and there were a few women, but not many. There was a deep murmur of conversation, and laughter rippled softly through the room.

Gianna felt the eyes of the men on her and Annamarie, as if they were speculating which of the girls Christopher was interested in. It's me, of course, you silly men, she thought. Can't you tell by the way he holds my arm?

Christopher guided them between the tables, smiling and speaking to some of the diners as they passed. He led the girls to a table near the wall. His friends were waiting for them. Ted Hall, a scholarly looking man with a crewcut and horn-rimmed glasses. And his fiance, Sara Lorensen, blonde and pretty. There was also Jim Wong from Formosa, and Spencer Williams from Liverpool, England.

Dinner was both pleasant and interesting. Gianna was fascinated by the variety of backgrounds. She asked question after question. What was it like in Formosa, in Liverpool? What were they going to do after their ordination?

Annamarie gave her a nudge under the table. Gianna laughed. "I have the feeling I'm asking too many questions. But it really is so interesting, meeting people from all over the world."

They were all smiling at her. Jim Wong said, "You might say, Gianna, that we're like ships that pass in the night. In a few months we'll all be going off in different directions, maybe never to meet again."

Then Ted said, "You girls are in for a special treat tonight. Sara brought her violin, and after we give you a tour of the school we're going to have a little concert. Sara and Chris."

Annamarie turned to Christopher. "You mean we're finally going to hear you play the piano?"

"Don't sound as if you're expecting something fantastic from me. Sara here is the musician. I'm just her accompanist."

"Don't listen to him," Sara said. "He's better than I am. He likes to make believe he doesn't play well."

After the tour of the school, Gianna and Annamarie settled down with the others in comfortable armchairs arranged in a circle around the baby grand piano in the recreation hall. The gay, lovely music of "Vienna Woods" filled the room, and the lamplight kept changing shadows on Christopher's face and hands. Gianna didn't notice Sara at all.

She felt happy and at peace with the world. Outside the night was cold and bitter, and the winds crashed against the curtained, latticed windows. But here in this great, beautiful room with the paneled walls and glittering chandeliers was a world that was new to her.

The world of Christopher Branning. Beautiful music and interesting people who cared, really cared, what happened to other people. These people who had come together from different parts of the world, and who in a short time would branch off again to fulfill dreams, to make a better life for those who were yet strangers to them.

She glanced sideways at Annamarie, and in that moment saw something she had never seen before, her sister's feelings thrust to the surface, naked, revealing. Saw the way her sister was watching Christopher and fingering her engagement ring at the same time.

Gianna was filled with sudden despair. Why had she failed to see it? Of course. That was why Annamarie was so edgy lately. Whether she knew it or not, she was in love with Christopher.

And what about him? Gianna remembered now so many things that had made no impression at the time. The way his hands sometimes lingered on Annamarie's shoulders when he helped her into her coat, the way his eyes followed her across the room.

Was it possible he was in love with Annamarie? Of course. Her sister was the reason they were here tonight.

In the revelation there was a sharp jolt to Gianna's

pride. She had really believed she was the one Christopher cared about.

The moment of hurt pride passed and she was suddenly afraid for her sister. It had been different when she thought she was the one Christopher wanted. Then it had seemed light and romantic, and impossible anyway.

But with Annamarie it was something else. Where would it all end? Where *could* it all end? Could Annamarie really go away with him to South America? And what about Sal?

Christopher and Sara ended their little concert with some selections from *The Merry Widow.* Their friends applauded enthusiastically and gathered around the piano.

Annamarie said softly, her eyes shining, "That really was beautiful." Gianna hoped Christopher wouldn't read the rapture in her sister's face.

Ted said, "Listen, Chris, there's a party over at the Y tonight. Why don't you and the girls come with us? We're going to dance to records and maybe play charades. We'll have a lot of fun. How about it?"

Christopher looked at the girls. "Well? It's up to you."

Annamarie said quickly, "Yes, we'd love to."

In the ballroom at the Y, couples were dancing to records, and there was a table with a punch bowl. Here, too, brilliantly lighted chandeliers shone down on highly polished floors, and tall, latticed windows were curtained against the windy winter night.

Annamarie drifted into Christopher's arms, and Jim

Wong asked Gianna to dance. Gianna thought, If Papa could see me now, dancing with a Chinese boy!

She liked Jim Wong. They had so much to talk about. "I never knew anyone from Formosa before," she said. "I hope you don't mind all my crazy questions."

He smiled, and she thought he was really quite nice looking with his smooth golden skin and very white, even teeth. "That makes us even," he said. "I never met a girl who was going to be an archaeologist."

She looked around her at the other divinity students dancing with their girlfriends and wives. "I've really enjoyed meeting Christopher's friends and seeing the school. My sister has, too."

"Yes, I've noticed that. I see your sister enjoyed coming. But not for Chris's friends or the school."

She followed his eyes and saw Christopher and Annamarie dancing together. He was holding her close and she had her face against his shoulder. Sometimes she looked up at him and he smiled down at her and pulled her closer, whispering something in her ear.

"How long has this been going on?" Jim Wong asked curiously.

"How long has what been going on?"

"Your sister and Chris."

"It hasn't."

He laughed. "You mean they've just discovered each other?"

"I don't know. My sister is engaged to a soldier who's off in the South Pacific."

"I see."

"She and Chris like each other. That's all. He's been a very close friend to both of us since he came to work with us."

His smile deepened as he danced her over to the punch bowl. "Yes, of course."

Annamarie and Christopher joined them at the table. Christopher said, "Gianna, I hope you're having fun. Is Jim Wong treating you all right?"

"Oh, yes, he's treating me fine."

She wondered if he had talked Jim Wong into keeping her company so that he could have Annamarie to himself. She looked at him closely. He seemed so different tonight. Younger, even carefree. His face was flushed and his eyes shining. She wanted to tell him to forget her sister, before they were both sorry. But she knew it was already too late.

In the ladies' room a short while later, as she watched Annamarie comb her long dark hair and put on fresh lipstick, Gianna said, "We ought to be going home soon. It's getting late. Papa will be furious."

Annamarie laughed at her. "Listen, Gianna, we're having such a wonderful time, let's not spoil it. Papa isn't happy about this anyway. And you did remind me that I was twenty-one, remember?"

Gianna stared at her. "Well, it is only this one time."

A shadow passed over her sister's face. The lights dimmed in her eyes. "Perhaps for you, Gianna. Not for me."

"Annamarie, do you realize what you're doing, what you're getting into?"

Her sister's answer was soft. "Yes, Gianna, I know."

Some of the divinity students cornered Christopher and asked him to play the piano. He was reluctant. "Well, just one thing."

He sat down at the baby grand, and Annamarie stood behind it, leaning forward, her elbows resting on the polished wood, her chin in her hands. Her eyes met his and they smiled at each other, and he played "Smoke Gets In Your Eyes."

When he finished the one song, he rose from the bench and said, "Put another record on, let's dance some more."

"Via Con Dios" filled the huge room, and his arms reached out for Annamarie. The other couples, too, drifted off in each other's arms.

"A penny for your thoughts," Jim Wong's soft voice cut in.

Gianna was startled. "What? Oh, I'm sorry. I guess my thoughts were elsewhere."

She danced with him, and then she saw that Christopher and Annamarie were no longer dancing. They were sitting in a shadowed corner by themselves, holding hands and murmuring.

Christopher walked them to the front door, while Sara and Ted waited for him in the car. "I hope you had a good time tonight, Gianna," he said. "I feel I neglected you."

"You didn't neglect me, Chris. And I did have a wonderful time."

"I'm glad. How about you, Annamarie?"

Annamarie's eyes were glowing in the darkness.

"Yes, I had a wonderful time, too, Chris."

Words. Silly, meaningless words, Gianna thought. They have a million things to say to each other, a lifetime to catch up on, and I am in the way. But if I go inside without her, then Mama and Papa will be furious.

For a moment Christopher and Annamarie stood there staring at each other, not speaking. Then, just as Gianna started to unlock the front door, Christopher leaned over and kissed Annamarie and smiled at her. "Tomorrow?" he whispered.

She clung to him for a moment. "Yes, tomorrow."

When they opened the front door Maria looked at the little clock on the table. "My, that was a long dinner." She was crocheting on Annamarie's bedspread.

"They were having a party after dinner, so they invited us," Gianna said.

Maria's eyebrows lifted, knowingly. She stared at Annamarie's face. "A party? No wonder you wore such a fancy dress."

"We didn't know about it beforehand. Christopher didn't either," Gianna said. "It was unexpected."

Maria's thick-knuckled hands rested in the lacy depths of the bedspread. "I hope this is finished."

And Cesare, who had been silent until now, said, "Yes, this is finished. Right?"

"What is there to finish?" Annamarie said lightly. "Well, I don't know about you, Gianna, but I'm tired. I'm going to bed."

In their room they lay still and unsleeping in the darkness.

"Annamarie?"

"Yes?"

"What did you and Chris mean about tomorrow?"

Silence for a moment. Then: "I'm meeting him downtown tomorrow afternoon. We're having supper together."

"Why, Annamarie?"

The answer came in the darkness, the answer she had already known. "We love each other," Annamarie said softly.

"Love! How can you love him just like that?"

"Not just like that, Gianna. It's been happening for awhile. Or didn't you notice anything?"

"But you hardly know him. And you're engaged to someone else."

"I'll tell you a secret. When I see Christopher tomorrow I will take off this ring."

Gianna thought of Sal far away, remembered the love in his eyes every time he looked at Annamarie. "But why did you get engaged in the first place if you didn't love Sal?"

Annamarie sighed. "Oh, you know how it was. I was feeling low about Christmas, everything at home was so grim because of Eddy. And then Sal came home and suddenly life was bright and happy and exciting. It was so easy, so fast, Gianna, it seemed right at the time."

"You had too much pressure from Mama and Papa and Sal's mother."

"No, I can't blame them. I do love Sal, in a way. Can you understand that?"

"No."

"But what I feel for Christopher, that's very different."

"How do you know it's not like it was with Sal? Maybe you're turning to Chris because you're lonely and depressed."

"No, this is different."

"I noticed you didn't say anything to Mama and Papa."

"Not tonight. I'm so happy right now I don't want to spoil it. I want to go to sleep tonight with this happiness still perfect. Tomorrow night I will tell them. After we've had a long talk about our future and made our plans."

"This happiness isn't going to stay perfect, you know. Mama and Papa aren't going to accept Christopher, especially with Sal overseas. And are you really thinking what marrying Christopher will mean?"

"Yes, I know. It will mean going to South America with him. It will mean giving up my family."

"You'll be doing all the giving up, he has nothing to give up. Can you really do that and be happy? You don't even know what kind of a mission he's going to. It's off in some awful jungle."

"As long as he's there I'll be happy. That's all I want, to be where he is. Besides, Sara is giving up a promising career to marry Ted and be a small-town minister's wife."

"That's different. She's the same religion and she isn't engaged to someone else. Oh, I hope you know what you're doing. I wish you could give it some more time, not rush into it. I mean, why can't you wait for awhile?"

"How long can I wait? He's leaving in June. I want to go with him. And how can I go out with him now and still wear Sal's ring?"

"I can just see his mother when you tell her. She's going to be heartbroken."

"And me, Gianna. What about me? Don't I have a right to marry the man I love? And do you think this doesn't hurt me? Do you think it's easy for me?"

In the darkness Gianna mused, "It's funny how prophetic Mama was last night. She said her intuition told her you would regret this dinner."

"She had it mixed up. I won't regret it. She will."

17

Maria was crocheting on Annamarie's bedspread, and occasionally she glanced nervously at the living-room clock. "When did Annamarie say she'd be back?"

Gianna didn't look up from her book. "She didn't say, Mama. Maybe she stayed over for the second show. Maybe the other girl who sells bonds didn't show up."

She wasn't lying. Annamarie was going to sell bonds at the theater, as she always did on Sundays. That was where Christopher was meeting her.

Gianna was edgy. She had the feeling the world was going to crash in on all of them very soon, when Annamarie returned. She was relieved when the doorbell rang. But only briefly. The visitor was Sal's mother.

Flushed and breathless, Mrs. Donato lowered her huge bulk into an armchair. "I'm worried," she said. "I haven't heard from Sal for two weeks. I wondered if Annamarie had a letter."

"No, she hasn't heard in about that time either, the last time she called you," Maria said.

"I hate to bother you like this. It's just that I'm so worried."

Maria, having gone through her own sorrows from

the war, could understand. "I know. But sometimes the mail gets bottled up someplace. Maybe it couldn't get through. How about a cup of coffee? Gianna, put a pot of coffee on, will you?"

Gianna, glad to leave the room, went out to the kitchen. As she took down the cups and saucers and set out a plate of Stella D'Oro biscuits, she heard Mrs. Donato ask, "Where is Annamarie?"

"At the movies selling bonds," her mother answered.

Mrs. Donato sighed. "Oh, what a girl my son has! I'm sure it makes him happy to know all the time she gives to selling bonds. It was a happy day when those two started going together. I can hardly wait for this terrible war to be over so my boy can come home and they can be married."

Oh, yes, Gianna thought, Sal would really be proud if he knew she's in love with someone else and is taking off his ring today! How was Annamarie going to explain to these two mothers who loved Sal so much? How could they ever understand?

Mrs. Donato's nervous rambling ceased abruptly, as if she had suddenly remembered that Maria's son would not return from the war. "I'm sorry. Stop me if I talk too much. It's just that I worry so."

Maria reassured her. "What's a mother if she doesn't worry over her children?"

It was not till ten o'clock that Annamarie returned, looking pale and emotionally drained. She was still wearing Sal's ring.

Maria was concerned. "You look exhausted. Why

did you stay for the second show? Can I get you something? Some soup, some coffee, something to eat?"

"No, Mama, I'm all right. Just tired. I think I'll go right to bed." Gianna caught the despair in her voice.

Maria kissed Annamarie. "Sal's mother stopped by. She was worried because she hadn't gotten a letter from Sal lately. I told her you didn't either. The mail probably didn't get through. You'll both get a bunch of letters at the same time, you'll see. Well, you go to bed. You sure you don't want a cup of tea or something? Did you eat anything tonight?"

"Yes, I had a sandwich."

When Annamarie had gone upstairs, Maria wiped tears from her eyes and sighed heavily. "This war, this war, will it never end so that mothers can stop worrying and young people get on with their lives? You think it was easy to tell Mrs. Donato everything was probably all right? What an actress you have to be these days. Pretend, pretend, make believe everything is going to be all right.

"Gianna, I get so tired of keeping up a front for everybody when every bone in my body is aching with grief. I want to cry for everybody. Especially my Annamarie."

"Annamarie, Mama?"

"Yes, Annamarie. Don't you see the way she goes around? The way she looked tonight? She doesn't say it but she's worried sick over Sal. You could see it tonight especially. She wasn't keeping up the pretenses tonight. It was all there, in her eyes, in her face."

Maria picked up her crocheting again. Her fingers moved like lightning, thc silver needle flashing in the lamplight. There was a kind of vengeance in those moving hands, an anger and grief she was trying to assuage.

"I'm going to bed," Gianna said. "Why don't you go, too?"

"No, I'll wait for your father. He'll be home from the club soon. Besides, I couldn't even go to sleep now."

Gianna closed the bedroom door behind her. She switched on the lamp on the bureau.

"Turn it off," Annamarie said sharply. She was lying face down on her bed.

"Why?"

"Because—oh, never mind. You can leave it on."

Gianna sat on the edge of her sister's bed and took her hand. "What happened, Annamarie?"

Annamarie turned over. She had been crying. Her eyes were red and her face blotchy. "Well, you worried about me for nothing. I won't be marrying Christopher anyway."

"I don't understand."

"He said we had to end it, that's all."

Gianna remembered the way Christopher had looked at Annamarie only last night, the way he'd held her close to him when they were dancing, as if he wanted never to let her go. "But last night—"

"He said we got carried away by circumstances last night."

"But I can't believe that! I mean—the way he looked at you, the way he danced with you. Everybody else noticed it."

"Well, it's over, that's all. And if that's the way he wants it, I'm not throwing myself at him. I know what he's thinking. I'm Catholic and he wants a Protestant wife."

"Maybe he's trying to protect you from getting hurt."

"Hurt? What am I now?" Annamarie started to cry again.

Gianna slipped an arm around her. "This hurt will pass, the other would be for a lifetime. You'll see. He'll go away and you'll forget you ever knew him."

The tears streamed down Annamarie's cheeks. "Oh, Gianna, I would have followed him to the ends of the earth! I would have given up everything just to be with him! I love him, Gianna!"

Gianna held her close and stroked the damp hair. "I know, I know. But it will pass. You'll forget. It will just take a little time."

"Forget him? When I see him every day?"

The next morning at school Gianna found out about the scholarships. She had won enough to carry almost all her expenses at college for the whole four years. She could hardly wait to tell Annamarie.

As she reached the door of the shop she could see Annamarie and Christopher having what seemed to be an argument. Her sister's eyes were blazing and she looked as if she had been crying.

Gianna opened the door, and the ringing of the little bell ended their discussion. They stared at her in numb silence.

Then Annamarie, flustered, said, "Hi, Gianna, you're early today."

"I'm sorry if I interrupted anything."

"It was nothing. My, you look bubbling. You must have had a good day at school."

Gianna put her books down and hung up her coat. Her good news didn't seem so happy any more. "I won the scholarships," she said. "They'll take care of most of my expenses for the whole four years."

Annamarie hugged her, her eyes misty. "Oh, that's great, Gianna. I'm so happy for you."

And Christopher squeezed her hand. "I'm glad for you, too, Gianna. I see great things ahead for you."

But she had lost interest in her own success. She was disturbed over the sadness that hung over the room. She looked at them and said, "All right, what's the matter? This air is so thick you could slice it. Did something happen that I should know about?"

Annamarie turned away and began to rearrange a table of books. Christopher said, "I'm leaving the Book Shoppe, Gianna."

Her world darkened. "Leaving!"

"Yes, at the end of the week."

"But—I don't understand! You're not being ordained until June."

"No, but I have a lot of studying and preparations

before then, and I have a chance to work at school. It will be easier for me."

She stared hard at him, trying desperately to hold back her tears. "I'll sure miss you, Chris." She flushed, aware she had meant to say "we."

Christopher said quietly, "I'll miss you, too, Gianna."

"I'll bring your *War and Peace* back tomorrow."

"No, I want you to keep it."

"But it was a special gift to you!"

"So now it's a special gift to you. I want you to finish it. Will you?"

She nodded. "Yes, I'll finish it."

He was looking past her at Annamarie, who stood staring out the windows now, her back to them, her arms folded across her chest.

"But you'll come in and see us, won't you? I mean, you won't just drop out of our lives? We will keep in touch? I mean—I want to know about your mission. I'll want to know all about it."

"Yes, we'll keep in touch."

Annamarie left the room in tears. Gianna looked at Christopher and saw the terrible sadness in his eyes.

"It will be better if I go now," he said.

"Better? For you, you mean?"

He shook his head. "No, for your sister. She could never be happy in my kind of life. She would have to give up everything she loved, everything that has always been dear to her. Do you understand what I'm saying?"

She nodded, feeling miserable herself. "I think so. You're saying you're in love with her but you don't want her to love you."

"Yes, that's right."

"But suppose—suppose it's too late, Chris? Suppose she already loves you?"

"No, it's not too late. If I go now—in a few months I'll be far away. She'll never see me again. It will be better that way. Sal will come back from the war and she will marry him and live happily ever after."

"You're sure?"

"Yes, I'm sure. And, Gianna—"

"Yes?"

"Of course you know we will not keep in touch. When I leave here it will be the end of our friendship."

"Yes, I know. I can't think why I said all those things about keeping in touch. That is the whole point of your leaving."

It was his last day at the shop, and now it was time to close. Gianna, returning from the rest room, found them together. She stepped back into the shadows, not wanting to interrupt.

Annamarie was in tears again and Christopher was trying to comfort her.

"I don't want you to go, Chris."

"It's better this way."

"Why is it better?"

"You know as well as I do where it's heading."

"But we love each other!"

His face blanched in the dull glow of the night lights. "No," he said. "We've just been thrown together and enjoyed each other's company and been very good friends. That's all it is, all it ever was. Look, I'll go away and you'll forget I ever existed. And when Sal comes back from the war you'll marry him and have a home and family here where you belong and forget you ever knew me."

She smiled bitterly through her tears. "You have my life all planned, don't you? Just like my mother and father. Everyone has it all planned, and no one's asking me what I want, no one's giving me a choice."

He touched the diamond on her finger. "If I were to return in ten years I'm sure I'd find you quite happily married, and probably one of your children would be making his First Communion."

"Why don't you say what you really mean? That you can't afford to fall in love with a Catholic girl, because it will interfere with your own plans?"

In his brief silence Gianna sensed the terrible struggle going on inside him. And then he made the decision. He moved away from Annamarie. "Yes, that's true, of course. There would be difficulties."

Annamarie turned cold. "Yes, now it's in the open and I understand."

She reached for her coat, and when Christopher tried to help her she pushed his hands away angrily. "Gianna!" she called out. "Are you ready yet?"

The door of the Book Shoppe locked behind the three of them, the brass knocker gleaming in the darkness. A cold wind blew over from the Green.

Gianna looked up at Christopher and realized she would probably never see him again. She remembered all the wonderful conversations they had had, the books he had brought her from the school library, all his care and concern for her dreams, her future.

She kissed him lightly on the cheek. "Good-bye, Chris. I'll really miss you."

She remembered her fantasy of turning down his marriage proposal, but in the fantasy she had been lighthearted and philosophical in sending him away with no regrets. In real life it was harder to say good-bye to him.

Oh, Christopher, Christopher, she mourned silently. You will never know—no one will ever know—that you were my first love.

He gave her a brief hug. "I'll miss you, too," he said. "I'm sure some day I'll pick up a newspaper or a *National Geographic* and read about some archaeological expedition in Africa, and there will be your picture."

"Who knows?" She laughed shakily. "I may even get to South America. I'll look you up if I do."

He turned to Annamarie, who was staring at him with bitter eyes. "Good luck to you, too, Annamarie, in everything."

"Don't worry about me," she said icily.

He looked at her for one last moment, then turned quickly and hurried down Chapel Street toward the school, his collar turned up against the cold wind.

Annamarie said in a broken voice, "Let's go or we'll miss the bus."

She was silent all the way home. Gianna, sitting next to the window, saw her sister's reflection in the glass, and her heart ached for her. The veneer of anger and bitterness was gone now. In its place was a terrible desolation.

I know how you feel, Gianna wanted to cry out to her. I loved him, too.

At home Mrs. Donato was waiting for them, red eyed and weeping. She threw her arms around Annamarie.

"I just got a wire," she sobbed heartbrokenly. "Sal's missing in action."

18

The theater manager smiled at Gianna and Annamarie as they turned in the cigar boxes of money and unsold bonds. "You had a good afternoon," he said. "See you next week."

From the warm darkness of the theater they stepped out into the bright sunshine of the May afternoon.

"It's too nice to go right home," Gianna said. "Let's go over to the Green and sit for awhile, maybe feed the pigeons."

Annamarie shrugged indifferently. "If you want to."

The trees were in full leaf now. The sunshine streamed like jeweled light through the branches of the elms and cast a golden glow on everything it touched. Over in Malley's department store, across from the Green, the shop windows were full of summer fashions.

Gianna bought a bag of popcorn from the vendor on the corner, and she and Annamarie found an empty bench in the upper block, behind Trinity Church. The pigeons flocked around them, cooing, watching hungrily. Gianna fed them and tried to make conversation.

But as usual Annamarie was quiet and withdrawn.

She had changed so much in the last few months. She had lost weight, and her thinness gave her a sallow, fragile look. When Christopher had stepped out of her life her world came to a standstill. She moved through the days like an empty shadow, lonely, introspective.

Sometimes Gianna would find her lying face down on her bed in the darkened bedroom, listening to classical music.

"Why do you listen to that music if it reminds you so much of him?" Gianna would ask.

And Annamarie would answer, "Because it's all I have of him."

"Think about Sal, Annamarie. Think about saying a few prayers for him. He's the one who needs it."

"Don't you think I know? Don't you think I feel guilty enough? Can you understand what it's like to have to face his mother all the time? To have her—and all the family—believe that I'm really grieving over Sal? It's agony. I can't take much more of it. One of these days I'm just going to crack up. I know it."

Gianna threw popcorn to some newly arrived pigeons at the fringe of the flock around their bench. "They sure are hungry," she said.

"They're lucky," Annamarie commented. "They have nothing else to think about."

She stared at a young soldier and his girl as they passed, arm in arm, laughing into each other's eyes. And in Annamarie's eyes was an unmasked longing.

Then something changed in her face. Suddenly. In her eyes was a quickening, a new flush of warmth in her sallow cheeks.

Curiously Gianna followed her sister's gaze and saw what had brought her back to life again. A tall, familiar figure was coming down the walk from the direction of Yale, the spring sunshine dancing in his blond hair. Gianna's heart, too, quickened.

Christopher, casually dressed in slacks, a pullover tweed sweater, and old sneakers, had returned to them. By some quirk of fate he, too, had decided it was a nice day to walk through the Green. At first he looked startled, flustered. He stopped in front of them.

"Hi, girls, this is a nice surprise."

Gianna returned his smile and greeted him warmly, but Annamarie merely murmured a cool hello. Gianna slid down to the edge of the bench. "Sit down, Chris."

He sat beside Annamarie, who ignored him and stared at some children playing across the walk. Christopher glanced down at her engagement ring. "I see the engagement is still on," he said quietly.

Her face shadowed. "Sal is missing in action. For a long time now."

"Oh, I'm sorry."

She looked up at him finally, and whatever her inner emotions were, her voice was cool and controlled. "How are things with you, Chris?"

"Hectic. The time is getting short."

"Yes, you'll be leaving soon, won't you?"

"In about a month."

An awkward silence followed, unspoken words heavy between them.

"We've sure missed you, Chris," Gianna said. "The shop hasn't been the same since you left."

Christopher looked away from Annamarie. "Did you ever finish *War and Peace?"*

"Yes. I loved it. Every page."

"I said you would, didn't I? And how are things going at school?"

"I'm going to be valedictorian."

His eyes lit up with pleasure. "Well, I knew you could do it. I'm very proud of you."

It was as it had been in the beginning, Gianna thought. She and Chris discussing school. But it could never be the same again. Even on this sunny spring day the happiness was gone from their friendship.

Annamarie stood up. "We have to be getting home," she said. Her voice was still cool and unemotional, but her eyes betrayed her. They were brimming over with love and despair.

Christopher, too, stood up, close to her, almost touching her. "I'd like to talk to you, Annamarie." He took her hands in his, his blue eyes searching hers. "Do you think you'd like to talk to me?"

She stared at him for one long moment, as if struggling with an inner decision. "Yes, there are some things we need to say to each other." She turned to Gianna. "You don't mind, do you?"

Seeing their hands entwined, and the love in their faces, Gianna thought, It never ended with these two.

"No, of course not," she said. "I'll go home by myself. But what shall I tell Mama? She'll want to know what happened to you."

"Tell her"—Annamarie was smiling up at Christopher now—"tell her I met an old friend and that I'll be home pretty soon."

Christopher said, "It's really great seeing you again, Gianna, and I'm very happy about the way things are going with you."

"Thanks, Chris. It was good seeing you again, too."

The two walked away, into the sunshine of the May afternoon, arm in arm now, and as she looked after them Gianna had the sure feeling that they would not be separated again if they could help it. And she marveled at the fate that had made her think of sitting on the Green on this particular afternoon. Suppose she and Annamarie had gone straight home as they always did? Perhaps Annamarie and Christopher would never have met again.

In one way Gianna was happy for her sister, remembering the way Annamarie had been looking and acting these last two months. But then she remembered all the complications, and it was impossible to stay happy.

Annamarie will pay a terrible price for this love, she thought. All of us will. With a heavy heart she headed for home.

The kitchen was warm and the air heavily laced with the pungent smells of steaming cabbage and simmering *fava* beans. Her mother was frying garlic in a small black pan. Frank Sinatra was singing on the radio.

"Where's Annamarie?" her mother asked.

"She met an old friend," Gianna answered.

Her heart pounded as she hoped her mother

wouldn't ask her who the old friend was. But Maria was too busy turning the garlic before it burned. She just said, "Good. Maybe it will cheer her up some. She's been so depressed lately. I wish we'd hear something about Sal. His mother dropped by and we had a cup of coffee. Oh, Dominique called. She said to call her when you got a chance. Something about school."

Annamarie came home about eight-thirty. She was not the same girl who had left the house earlier. Happiness glowed in her radiant face and shining eyes.

Her mother stared suspiciously at her. "Who was the friend Gianna said you met?"

"Christopher Branning, Mama."

Maria's face paled. Instinctively she glanced at Annamarie's hand and saw the engagement ring was missing. "Your ring—where's your ring?"

Cesare looked up from his newspaper, waiting for the answer. When Annamarie hesitated, Maria became angry. "Where's your ring? Did you lose it?"

"No, I didn't lose it, Mama. I took it off."

"Took it off!" Cesare shouted, the newspaper dropping suddenly to the floor. "What you mean, you took it off?"

Annamarie sat down on the sofa. Her radiance was gone now. "I'm not engaged to Sal any more. I'm going to marry Christopher."

Her parents were pale and shaking. They stared at her incredulously.

"What you mean—marry him?" her father shouted. "You're engaged to Sal!"

"Not any more, Papa."

Maria's face was flushed with anger. "The missionary? You're going to marry the missionary?"

"Yes, Mama. As soon as he's ordained. In about a month. He's going to South America and I'm going with him as his wife."

Her mother was staring at her as if she had committed a terrible crime. "And all the time I thought you were mourning over poor Sal."

"It was a mistake getting engaged to Sal. I wasn't really in love with him."

"What you mean you weren't in love with him?" Cesare demanded. "You mean you stopped when you find he's missing?"

"Oh, Papa, no! I've been in love with Chris for a long time, for months. It had nothing to do with Sal's being missing."

"But you're engaged to Sal!" He still could not accept the truth.

"Not any longer, Papa. It's over."

His eyes were bitter as he glared at her. "Too bad you can't tell him. And how you tell that to his mother who's all the time saying to everyone in the neighborhood how lucky her son is to have such a fine girl waiting for him when he comes home, how faithful, how she's always selling bonds to help the war end faster so he can come home and marry her? Only this afternoon she was here in this room praising you, telling us how much she loved you. How you tell all this to her? How you face her now? How do we face her?"

"If Sal was all right, that's bad enough," her mother broke in. "But to break your engagement when he's missing, maybe he's sick somewhere and is thinking only of you—maybe he's hurt—"

"Oh, Mama, stop it!" Annamarie was crying now. "You don't know how terrible I feel about it. But I can't help it. I didn't love Sal."

"Stupid, you're stupid!" Cesare yelled. "You be sorry for the rest of your life!"

"I know what I'm doing, Papa."

"All right, all right. So you're a big girl now. I try to show you the right way, your mama she try to bring you up right. But you're stupid. From now on it's your own mistake, all by yourself. So you think you know what you want? So go live your own life. But just remember, when you go to pick up the pieces, remember how we try to stop you."

Silence filled the room, broken only by the ticking of the clock on the wall. "And everybody knows you're engaged to Sal and he's missing. Everybody knows." His eyes were black with fury. "Well, I tell you something. The day you marry this—this—missionary I close the door in your face forever. Forever! You think I joke? Well, I mean every word. When I say something I never take it back. Christ Himself couldn't make me take it back. You understand what I'm saying?"

She stared at him unbelievingly at first, meeting the contempt in his eyes. Then she dried her tears and stood up. In a very cold voice she said, "Oh, yes, Papa, I do understand. I understand very well."

She ran blindly from the room. Cesare, too, stamped out angrily, the cellar door slamming behind him a moment later.

Maria started to cry. "We don't have enough sorrow in this house, she has to do this to us!"

Gianna, feeling helpless in the midst of all the passion and misery, put an arm around her mother and tried to console her. "Mama, she hasn't done anything to you."

Her mother drew away from her. "What do you mean—she hasn't done anything to us? She is blackening our name, bringing dishonor into our house. We will never be able to hold up our heads again in this neighborhood. Everyone will say what is true. As soon as Sal went overseas she started looking for someone else, and as soon as he was missing she just turned her back on him completely. She couldn't wait for him. His mother is pining away her life over him and Annamarie couldn't even be faithful to him for a little while."

It had become more than a broken engagement. It was now a matter of family honor and pride.

"It's not like that at all, Mama."

"Then what else is it? You tell me."

"Everybody always pushed her toward Sal. She was never sure. Even after she got engaged she wasn't sure.

He came home at Christmas when she was feeling sad over Eddy—the way we all were—and he was so full of joy and life, and everything happened so quickly.

"But she has been in love with Christopher for months now. I've seen it firsthand, Mama. And if you saw them together, if you saw how they love each other, you'd know it was something beautiful, not ugly the way you and Papa are making it out to be."

"Then why did he leave the store and not see her again if he was so much in love with her?"

"He wanted to spare her all this. He knew it would be like this."

"Well, at least he was right about that."

"Well, Mama, if she's going to marry him you just have to accept it."

Her mother's lips tightened grimly. "I don't have to accept nothing. You heard your father. He'll close the door on her forever if she marries this—this missionary."

"And you, Mama?"

Tears streamed down her mother's face. Suddenly Maria looked very old. "I have to live with your father."

Gianna closed the door of the darkened room where Annamarie lay face down on her bed. She sat down beside her sister.

"I could have told you it would be like this."

Annamarie blew her nose. "You didn't have to tell me. I knew. And Christopher did, too. He said that was one of the main reasons he tried to end it. He knew how close I was to the family and how they would react. He thought I'd be miserable."

"He was right about that, you know."

Annamarie's voice changed in the darkness. "No, he was wrong. Because you see when I'm with him that's all that matters. I don't care about anything else. If I can be with him, share his life, then I can accept all of this."

"Well, maybe Papa will soften up after you're actually married. After all, he loves you, he's only looking for you to be happy."

"No," Annamarie said bitterly, "he'll never change. Even if he knows he's wrong he will never admit it, never."

There was a tap on the door and Maria came into the bedroom. She left the door open, and the hall light streamed softly behind her. She sat down on Annamarie's bed beside Gianna.

"Look," she said quietly, "don't rush into anything. Take some time to think this over."

"There's nothing to think over, Mama. I'm going to marry Christopher."

"Oh, yes, there is a lot to think over. You better stop and think what you are doing to your whole life. For if you go with this missionary you will decide what your whole life will be like. Right now you think it's all moonlight and roses and romance, like the story books. But real life is very, very different, my child. It is not something you rush into, a marriage like this."

"I love him, and that's all that's important. Didn't you love Papa so much that you would have gone anyplace in the world just to be with him?"

Silence filled the room. And Annamarie was sorry she had asked the question. Of course it had not been that way with her mother. Her marriage with Cesare had been arranged by Nonna. Love had come with the years, gradually. If in the beginning he had wanted her to go off to some distant country the marriage would have been unthinkable.

"Love is something that grows with the years," Maria said now. "With the children, with sharing the good times and the bad. That's what real love is. Not like you think. This love you talk about is the kind that doesn't last. It dies after awhile. You'll see."

Annamarie's face was flushed with anger. "No, I won't see."

Her mother looked at her in sorrow. "Yes, you'll see. And you know when you'll really feel it? When you have your first child, maybe alone in some jungle somewhere, and you can't show it to your mother and father, and you can't even baptize it in your own church.

"That's when you will really know what you have done to yourself and your family."

Gianna went looking for her father. She hadn't heard him go out so she knew he must still be in the house.

She found him in the cellar. A naked bulb shone

down harshly on him as he sat on an upturned wooden crate, his head in his hands. He had been drinking. The wine bottle was on the workbench next to some potted tomato seedlings. Her heart went out to him. He looked so alone, so beaten.

"Papa—"

He lifted his head, and there were tears in his reddened eyes. He glared at her. "Don't you tell me nothing about planting—about God—about Christ and the hereafter—you don't tell me nothing!"

He stood up, and with a sudden angry sweep of his hand smashed the little pots of seedlings to the cement floor.

Gianna stared silently at the bits of broken clay, the scattered fragile stems. Her father's voice sent a chill through her as his heavy shoes crushed the young plants to pulp.

"I give my whole life to my children—to my family —and all I get is a broken heart! This is all I get for all the years I break my back working double shifts and dreaming for my children? In the end this is all it comes to—a broken heart!"

For once she had no words for him. She could only remember in aching longing that golden time not so long ago when life had seemed so perfect, when they had all been together as a family, loving each other, and her parents' beautiful dreams were all still possible.

19

A narrow stripe of sunlight found its way past the drawn shades and through the white net curtains and slanted across Gianna's face, compelling her to awaken. She heard the sparrows chirping and rustling in the nest they had built in the eaves of the house, and she snuggled under her blanket, peaceful and happy for the moment.

Until she remembered it was Annamarie's wedding day, and then the euphoria ended.

She turned on her side and looked over at her sister, this girl who would soon be Christopher's wife, this girl who would become a strange woman in a strange land. Annamarie looked so childlike in her sleep, so innocent and vulnerable. It was almost impossible to believe that this lovely, sleeping girl could have created so much heartache for so many people, especially herself.

Life at home had been miserable for the past month. Cesare had hardly spoken to any of them, and when he did it was always with anger. Maria had moved through her days with perpetually reddened eyes, her voice and manner edgy and reproachful.

Leonardo and Sal's mother no longer came to the

house. It was as if they couldn't bear to see Annamarie again, and in the neighborhood there were the whispers, the pointed remarks. The broken engagement was no secret. Every time Maria returned from the market, or even from Mass, she went around the kitchen slamming pans and doors, her face set in bitterness because of something someone had said or done.

"Good morning, Gianna." Annamarie was awake now. Gianna went to her bed and sat on the edge. She tried to smile.

"I can't believe this day is finally here."

"Well, it didn't come fast enough," her sister said bitterly. "The way things have been in this house lately, with Papa hardly speaking to me, and Mama always angry, and crying half the time, I wish I had left that first day. It's been hell, Gianna."

"I know."

"I can never forgive Papa for this, never."

"Never is a long time, Annamarie."

"Well, that's how long it will be then. Here I'm going away to another country, it will be a long, long time before I ever come back. And instead of sending me on my way wishing me joy and good luck, he's sending me away with a sad heart. Why, he never even met Chris. Even today, on our wedding day, he still refuses to meet him."

"Maybe he'll change his mind at the last minute."

"No, he won't change."

Gianna reached for her sister's hand. "Are you sure —absolutely sure? You'll never be sorry?"

Annamarie sighed. "Some day you'll love a man, and only then will you really understand."

The door opened, and Maria came in, carrying a large white box. "I have something for you," she said. She put it on Annamarie's bed and watched her open it.

Cradled in tissue paper was the crocheted bedspread. Annamarie flung her arms around her mother and cried, "Oh, Mama!" She knew only too well what it symbolized: hours and weeks and months of love and care and dreams.

"I made it for you," Maria said, her voice wavering. "I want you to have it. Maybe you'll remember me when you look at it."

"Oh, Mama, do you think I'll ever forget you?"

Maria held her daughter close. After a long moment she said, "This is your wedding day. It's not a day for tears. I want you to know that I love you and want you to be happy. Maybe I don't understand how you can do it this way. But you have a right to make your own choice. And just because your father has a black heart doesn't mean I'm the same. But you have to understand. I have to live with him. I can't go against him. That's why I can't go to your wedding."

"I know, Mama. I understand."

"But I'll be with you in spirit. You know that, don't you?"

"Yes, Mama, I know."

Maria looked at Rose's wedding picture on the bureau and sighed wistfully. "We were all so happy then. Everything was so beautiful in our life, so perfect."

"Life can't always be beautiful or perfect, Mama."

"I know. Don't I know."

"There is something I want to tell you that might make you a little happier, though. I didn't say anything before because I wasn't sure. We're going to be married by a priest too."

"And how are you going to manage that? What priest will marry you when you're also having a Protestant wedding?"

"Paolo has a friend, this young priest in Bridgeport. We went to see him one Sunday. We are going there today, when we leave here."

"So what good will that do?"

"You can feel that I was married as a Catholic. It might make Papa feel happier, too. Eventually."

"Right now I wouldn't dare even mention it," Maria said. She studied Annamarie's face. "And you. Will it make you happier?"

Her daughter stared back at her. "I guess it will, Mama." She hugged her mother tight. "I'll be back again. Missionaries get leaves. We'll come home on visits."

"Your father will never see you. You know that."

"Rose said we can stay at her house. We'll see you, anyway. In the meantime I'll write to you every week. I'll tell you everything I see and do. And you do the same for me. You will, won't you? I want to know everything, Mama. Every little detail. Tell me what you're cooking for supper, who got married in the neighborhood, everything."

"I will, I will."

When they went down to breakfast Maria said, "I made you some French toast. And some pork sausages."

She had put some rambler roses in a cutglass vase on the table. Cesare was reading the paper. He looked up at them and mumbled a reply to their good mornings, then resumed his reading.

They ate breakfast quietly, as Bing Crosby sang "My Blue Heaven" on the radio. Outside the sunshine was golden in the grass, and the air soft and lazy. In the kitchen was the warmth of the good smells of freshly brewed coffee and pancake syrup on French toast, but there was no warmth in the faces of the people at the table. Only a stillness, a waiting. A waiting for Cesare.

At last Annamarie said, "Papa, this is my wedding day. This is my last day home. Haven't you anything to say to me?"

He looked straight at her, and his black eyes were angry and brooding. "No," he answered. "I said what I wanted to say. There is nothing else."

"You can't even wish me good luck?"

He glared at her, his red brows knit together. "You make your own luck, good or bad. If you choose to ruin your life, that's your choice, not mine."

"That's all you have to say to me then, Papa?"

He rose from the table, almost menacing in his hugeness, and for a moment there was a softening in his face, a yearning. And then a return of the hardness. "No, I have nothing else to say."

He left the room, the kitchen door closing behind him.

The silence was of pain. Maria leaned across the table and her hands closed tightly over Annamarie's. "Don't expect him to change. He is like iron when he makes up his mind to something. You will break your heart if you expect him to change."

Annamarie said wistfully, "For just a second there I thought he really wanted to."

"That's the sad thing about your father. Even if he wants to he can't. It's part of his code of honor. It's the way his family was, the way he was brought up."

It was time to go. Rose and Mario stood at the front door, waiting.

Maria kissed Christopher and gave him a brief hug. "Make my daughter happy," she said.

"You don't have to worry about that," he reassured her, putting his arm around Annamarie, holding her close to his side. "I love your daughter. I'll always cherish her and do my best to make her happy. And we'll write to you." He hesitated awkwardly. "I only wish I could tell this to her father."

"You must try to understand and forgive him," Maria said. "He is from another world. His ways are different. It's not really his fault."

"Yes, I understand. Well, perhaps time and distance will change things."

Silence. Then Mario cleared his throat and said, "Do we have all the luggage now?"

Annamarie said, "Yes. We sent the other things ahead."

"I wrapped the spread in a box over there by the

sofa," Maria said. "But I could send it to you, if it would make it easier."

"Oh, no, Mama, I wouldn't take a chance on its getting lost," Annamarie protested. "It's too precious to me."

She looked at her mother now in sudden uncertainty, as if she were thinking, But you are getting old, my mother, and when will I ever see you again? Suppose I never see you again? Suppose—

She clung to her mother for one last time. "Try not to be sad, Mama. Just remember you haven't lost a daughter, you've gained a son."

They all laughed weakly, and then the wedding party moved out into the bright sunshine of the June morning. Annamarie reached over and pulled off a rambler rose from the side of the porch, and she glanced back at her mother's grim, tear-stained face in the open doorway. For a moment she looked as if she wanted to go back. Then Christopher put his arm around her, and she turned away and walked with him to the car.

Gianna, in a last moment of desperation, said, "Wait, I forgot something."

She ran breathlessly through the house and out the back door. Her father was sitting in the grape arbor, smoking a cigar.

"Papa," she said breathlessly, "Annamarie's leaving now. Won't you come out and say good-bye to her, at least wish her luck?"

He glared bitterly at her. "Go! Go to her wedding.

I told her I'd close the door on her face the day she married him. I don't take my word back for nobody—not even you!"

In his eyes the tears glittered.

As Gianna passed her mother at the front door, Maria murmured, knowingly, "I told you, you'll only break your hearts if you think you can make him change his mind."

Paolo was waiting for them at the school. He shook hands with Christopher, whom he had already met at the seminary one weekend. Then he hugged Annamarie, and when he saw her sudden tears, he put his hand under her chin.

"Hey, this is your wedding day. Forget everything else except that you love this man and he loves you. That's all that counts. And stop feeling guilty. You know what it says in the Bible about leaving your parents when you marry."

He turned to his other two sisters, who were going to stand up for Annamarie, and saw the mistiness in their eyes. "And I have something to say to you girls, too. Over here."

He took them to the other side of the room. "I know how you feel, how hard it is for you. But whatever tears you have, save them for when she's gone. She really needs your support right now. And especially your love and understanding. Let's all try to remember that this is a special day in her life. Let's make it as happy as possible. Promise?"

He was smiling, this brother who had his own life

to settle and usually didn't smile too much anyway. But in his smile they found the strength to swallow the pain.

"Promise," Rose agreed.

Gianna nodded. "I wish Julio and Valerie could have come, or at least Julio."

"Oh, Gianna," Rose said a little impatiently, "you know Valerie's baby is due any time now."

"Well, let's get on with the wedding," Paolo said.

There were white roses on the altar from Gianna and Paolo, and the little chapel was filled with divinity students and their girlfriends and wives, and a few of the professors. A warm breeze drifted in through the open, stained-glass windows. Narrow ribbons of sunshine lit up the varnish of the pews and turned the cross on the altar into a shining blaze of gold.

Jim Wong was best man, and Ted was performing his first marriage since his ordination. Sara played the wedding music on her violin.

Gianna thought her sister had never looked more beautiful than she did now, in her plain white dress, the candlelight gleaming richly in her long dark hair. And Christopher was handsome, no longer a divinity student but a minister, tall and dignified in a black clerical suit and starched white collar.

After the ceremony there was a brief reception in the recreation hall. Rose and Mario, with financial help from Julio, had arranged for a caterer to make sandwiches and salads, and the cooks at the school had baked a wedding cake, for which Rose had bought a miniature bride and groom.

"Don't forget to take the bride and groom with you," she reminded Annamarie. "And a piece of the cake, too. You can have it on your first wedding anniversary."

Sara played some love songs on her violin.

Gianna had become acquainted with many of the people at the school, for she had come here often with Annamarie and Christopher in the last month. She looked around her now at the great, lovely room with its paneled walls and crystal chandeliers and thought, This is the last time many of us will ever see each other again. We will go our separate ways, and in another few months most of us will be scattered around the country, even the world.

Jim Wong said, "I hear you're going to be valedictorian of your class, Gianna."

"Yes, that's right."

"You know, I'd like to write to you sometime."

"Sure, Jim. I'd love to hear about your church." Silently she reflected on the irony of a Chinese minister's wanting to write to her, Cesare's daughter.

The train had pulled in, and now their last moments of being together had come, and they could only stare at each other in silent desolation. All around them people were saying good-bye.

A sailor, looking hardly old enough to go off to war, was hugged by a tearful mother and an anxious father. His eyes sparkled with the excitement of embarking on a strange new adventure.

A young private, surely not more than nineteen,

stood with his child-like wife, who held a baby in her arms. The girl tried to be brave, but every once in awhile her sorrowful eyes would brim over with tears.

And there was an Army sergeant, older than the other two, who stood alone, without family or wife or girlfriend, and watched the others' good-byes. The battle stripes and Purple Heart on his chest were a silent explanation of why there was no joy of adventure in his lonely eyes.

"This is not the happiest of times for anybody," Paolo remarked. "How wonderful it will be when this war ends and all these boys can go back to living their lives again."

"Bridgeport, Stamford, New Rochelle, New York!" the conductor shouted. "All aboard!"

The sailor's parents hugged him for the last time, and he laughed at their fears and warnings and hurried away from them, almost impatient to get on with his adventure. The private held his wife close and now neither of them held back their tears. Then he cradled his baby son in his arms, studying the tiny face hungrily as if to memorize every feature, every crinkle. He handed the baby back to his wife, and, his arm tight around her, they walked slowly toward the train. The sergeant tossed away his cigarette butt and moved briskly up the train steps, the ache of loneliness in his face.

Gianna and Rose hugged Annamarie and their tears mingled. And as the sisters held each other they remembered all the years they had shared the same room and whispered in the darkness until Maria tapped on the wall and called out "Go to sleep!" Remembered all that sisters have to remember of each other, the tears and the laughter, the good times and the bad.

"It will be awhile but we will see each other again," Annamarie reassured them. "In the meantime we'll write. You tell me everything, you hear? How Mama and Papa are—what the baby is doing—everything. You, too, Paolo, and Mario."

Christopher had a special farewell for Gianna. "You keep up those dreams, little sister," he said. It was the first time he had called her that. It was what Eddy used to call her.

She held onto him for a moment, loving him still but in a different way now. "Oh, Chris, just make her happy. Just make it worth all she's giving up."

"You know I will, don't you?"

"Yes, I know."

"And, Gianna"—his blue eyes were full of concern now for her—"you must not brood over this situation. You have a life of your own to live. You're on the brink of an exciting new life, full of surprises, full of beautiful discoveries. That's what you must concentrate on now. Will you do that?"

"Yes, I will, Chris."

"And, Gianna, be good to your parents. They need you desperately. Especially your father."

"Yes, Chris."

They said good-bye again, but just as Annamarie

and Christopher started up the train steps, Annamarie turned back to her sisters and said, "Take care of Mama and Papa. And tell Papa—tell Papa—I love him."

The train started to pull out. Gianna walked along the side of it, waving to the two figures behind the grimy windows, the tears streaming down her cheeks. She saw also the pale, weary faces of the three servicemen looking out at the platform for the last time.

The train disappeared down the tracks, and she stopped waving. She sat down on a bench and buried her face in her hands.

She felt herself being enclosed in warm, masculine arms and she buried her face against Paolo's jacket, clinging to him.

"It's going to be all right," he said softly as he held her. "It's going to be all right, Gianna."

And then Rose was on the other side of her, stroking her hair. "Just remember, Gianna, remember what Mama always told us. We're a family, nothing can ever change that. And we've been through worse than this. Everything will turn out all right. You'll see. In time. Time changes a lot of things."

20

In the backyard the darkness was softened by moonlight glowing on the grass and wooden fences, and the fireflies flickered their tiny evanescent flames. The windows of the neighborhood were blacked out against the night, but from inside them drifted the sounds of radio music and a baby crying, and a woman's strident scolding of a child. There was the aroma of fresh-perked coffee, and down the block someone was practicing on a trumpet. Life went on in the neighborhood.

Gianna sat alone in the grape arbor, the evening breeze cool against her hot face, the night song of the crickets and the stirring of birds in the fruit trees accentuating her terrible loneliness and sorrow.

She was glad to be out of the house, away from the pervading sadness. For the sadness was there in the silence of a supper hastily eaten, in the slam of the back door as Cesare, sullen and withdrawn, left for the club. It was there in Maria's swollen red eyes and quivering lips as she washed the dishes with unusual roughness.

Gianna had tried in vain to ease her mother's heartache. She was grateful when Rose came to visit.

The walls of sorrow closed in on her. She thought

of Annamarie, far away by now, and wept. Wept for all the lost dreams, for all the lovely times that were gone forever.

All her life she had believed that no matter what happened to her, her family would be there, strong and united. That belief had sustained her through all the hard times, the physical discomforts, the tragedy of her brother's death.

But now she knew there was no more unity, and even the strength was diminishing, little by little. Nothing would ever be the same again.

Paolo came out and sat beside her. "What are you thinking about? Or would you rather not say?"

She started to tell him, but the words choked in her throat. He squeezed her shoulder. "I know how you feel. It's heartbreaking."

"He could have wished her luck. He could have bent that much."

"I know. But we have to try and understand. Papa's a victim of his own pride. It will cost him dearly, this holding onto ideals."

"I hope it does, I hope he suffers as he has made the rest of us suffer!" she said passionately.

"You don't mean that. He's your father and you love him no matter what his failings. But, Gianna, don't dwell on Annamarie. She's gone and you have your own life to live."

"Right now I don't care."

"Maybe not tonight. But tomorrow you must."

Gianna dried her eyes with her brother's handkerchief. "And you, Paolo? What about you?"

"And I will go on to the priesthood."

She remembered Christmas Eve when the family had seen him with Laura Riccitelli, remembered the happiness in his face, the laughter on his lips.

"But what about Laura?" The question popped out.

He stared into the darkness, and there was a moment of silence before he answered. "Laura and her family are moving to California this week. It's all over between us."

"I don't know whether to say I'm glad or sorry."

"You can be glad. Mama was always right when she said I was born to be a priest. I could never be anything else. And now I know."

In the house there was the ringing of the telephone, and shortly afterward Maria came rushing out the back door. "Gianna! Paolo! I have wonderful news!"

She hurried so much that she was laughing breathlessly when she reached the grape arbor.

"Mama! What is it? What's happened?"

"Valerie just had a baby boy! And they're going to name him Cesare! Wait till Papa hears."

Maria's voice was light and happy. "Oh, Mama, I'm so glad!" Gianna hugged her mother, finding comfort in the warm, loving arms.

The pain in Gianna's heart lifted as a new optimism swept through her. With a new baby in the family how could unhappiness possibly remain in the house? Everything would turn out all right one of these days. It always had with her family, and it always would. And some day there would be another telephone call, or perhaps a letter, from Annamarie announcing the birth of her first child, and maybe then Cesare could turn aside from his pride and let himself love his daughter once again.

"Rose and I are going to have a cup of coffee," Maria said. "Why don't you two come in and join us?"

Paolo rose from the bench. "Sounds good to me. Come on, Gianna."

"You go," Gianna said. "I'll be in in a minute."

Alone again in the darkness, she was no longer so unhappy. Paolo was right. She had her own life to think about, and the future was a bright, shining adventure. Soon she would leave this house, this neighborhood, to go out into the world and follow her own dreams.

She heard her father's footsteps in the alleyway and saw Cesare come around the corner of the house. Not seeing her in the darkness, he walked like an old man, slowly, his shoulders sagging, his feet heavy. Gianna's bitterness toward her father ended.

Oh, Papa, she thought, you dreamed such golden dreams for your children, and yet even with the dreams that came true your children are going away from you. Only Rose will stay really close to you. Soon there will be only you and Mama in the house.

She went to him and hugged him. "Papa, you came home early."

He struggled for words. She saw that he was touched and surprised by her unexpected show of affection. "So I came home early. I have to punch a time clock around here? I can't come home early to my own house?"

Hurt and defeated, he had come to the only place in the world that could heal him, his home.

"Oh, Papa, I have such great news for you! Wait till you hear. Valerie had a boy, Papa, and he's going to be named Cesare!"

In the darkness she saw a glint of tears. "A boy? Julio has a son?"

"Isn't that great, Papa?"

He tried to cover up his emotion. "What's so great? I told them I wanted a grandson. A grandson with my name."

He sniffed and cleared his throat. "Cesare Dellesanto, the second. So what are we doing out here? We have to celebrate."

Old dreams ended, Gianna thought, as the war would end, as the world of her father, with its ethnic and religious boundaries and its ironclad rules, would end. But in the moonlit darkness the fireflies were like tiny bright flames of hope, and the June night was fresh and young and exciting.

It was a time of new beginnings.

Epilogue—June, 1953

The limousine pulled up to the curb, and the passengers scrambled out to claim their luggage. As Gianna waited in line, the woman next to her remarked, "You look as if you had a good vacation with that beautiful tan."

Gianna smiled. "Not a vacation, really. I've been in Africa."

The woman's interest deepened. "Africa!"

"Yes, I'm an archaeologist."

"Oh, my, how exciting! You look so young. How long have you been there?"

"A few years. I'm working toward my doctorate."

"And you're coming home for a visit?"

Gianna's dark eyes glowed. "My family's having a reunion, the first time we've all been together in ten years. It's my parents' thirty-ninth anniversary."

"Well, have a wonderful time," the woman said, taking her suitcase from the driver.

Gianna decided to check her luggage and walk home from downtown.

The vast lawns of the Green lay verdant and peaceful in the sunshine of the June afternoon. The old men played checkers on the long wooden tables, and women and children threw popcorn and bread crumbs to the pigeons.

Gianna remembered all the times she had sat on those benches with Christopher, when she had shared her dreams and, unknown to him, the first romantic love of her life. There had been other men since then, but only recently had there been one she really loved.

She smiled, thinking how excited her parents would be when she told them she was going to marry a red-haired archaeologist named Dr. Terence O'Neill. In the past few years they had not been too thrilled over her scholastic accomplishments. To them she would never be completely successful until she married and had children.

"Don't wait too long," Maria was always warning. "Time passes, and all of a sudden you're too old to have a family."

It was going to be such a beautiful reunion, because Annamarie and Christopher were home with their three boys. Gianna had last seen them five years ago when they came to New Haven and stayed with Rose for a week. Maria had seen them then, too, but not Cesare.

That was the miracle—that Cesare's heart had softened at last toward the daughter on whom he had once closed his door. In a moment of weakness following an illness a few months ago, his longing overcame his fierce pride. Afterward he tried to retract his promise to see her, but it was too late. Maria was the strong one now.

And the others were home, too. Julio, a cardiologist in Boston now, was here with Valerie and young Cesare; and Paolo from his Indian mission in New Mexico.

Rose, of course, had never left the neighborhood. When Mario's mother died, leaving the three-family house to him, he and Rose had decided to stay, as the two rents from the house would pay for all their expenses and even make a little profit. And it was so close to Cesare and Maria that their five children were constantly running around the corner to visit their grandparents.

Gianna walked down east Chapel Street, through Columbus Park, and past St. Michael's. Now she was in the neighborhood again.

She passed the six-family tenement that had once belonged to her grandparents and remembered Nonna, in flowered apron and housedress, her white hair braided, dark eyes twinkling. And Nonno. How funny to think back on all the consternation he had caused when he returned from his trip to Italy with a beautiful eighteen-year-old bride.

"He won't live long enough to enjoy it," Cesare had predicted, his face red with laughter.

His prediction came true. Nonno died three months later and, to the unforgiving indignation of Zia Louisa, left everything he owned to his bride, who shortly afterward married a handsome young construction worker.

Across the street was the tenement in which Dominique and Muriel had lived. Dominique, who was in and out of love a dozen times during the war, was there with warmth and compassion when Sal Donato, bitter, disillusioned, and unwell, returned from three years of internment in a Japanese prisoner-of-war camp. She helped him find his way back to normal living, and in the process they fell in love and were married. Sal now owned a plumbing supply business, and they had a Cape Cod in the suburbs and three children. Gianna looked forward to seeing them again. She and Dominique had remained good friends despite the changes in their lives.

As for Muriel, she lived in Arizona, was married to a lawyer, and had a three-year-old son. Once, after the war, she came to New Haven for a visit and had a reunion with Gianna and Dominique. Since then there had just been exchanged Christmas cards with letters enclosed.

And far down the street was Zio Luigi's tenement. It was sad to think how he had died several years ago in an automobile accident, mourned only by Maria, who had never judged his way of life. The rest of his family remembered him only with scorn, particularly when it was learned that he left everything he owned to the church.

"That figures," Zia Louisa said caustically. "He thought he could buy his way into heaven and die with a better conscience."

Dear Zia Louisa. She was getting old now and was much fatter than before. Her husband had died a year ago but she hardly seemed to miss him because her life was so full of children, grandchildren, and great-grandchildren.

Gianna stood in front of her father's house, smiling to herself at the way, after all these years, she still thought of it as her father's and not her mother's as well. Brainwashed, from years of growing up believing it was completely a man's world.

She closed the gate behind her and felt like a very young girl again, the outside world far away. No matter where she went, home would always be this small gray house sandwiched in between the tenements, its windows sparkling in the sunlight. At the side of the tiny front porch, where she had so often curled up with the *National Geographic* in one hand and a heel of Italian bread in the other, the rambler roses were blooming, as they had on that unforgettable day when Annamarie left home to be married.

From the open windows drifted the flavorful aroma of her mother's cooking. She smiled. Lasagna, of course. What good Italian family would have a family reunion without lasagna? And chicken with garlic and parsley, the smell of it rich and pungent in the June air. Gianna could imagine all the cooking and baking that her mother and Rose had done these last few days. And her mother would have waxed the floors and washed all the curtains and draperies.

"Wait till you see the house now," Maria had written. There was a new refrigerator from Julio, and Mario had installed ceramic tile in the kitchen and bathroom. And, of course—the television set.

Gianna heard the low murmur of voices in the backyard. And children's laughter. She hurried through the alleyway. No one saw her at first, and she stood still and looked on the scene as if it were a movie.

Her father was sitting on the bench in the grape arbor, surrounded by his family. She hadn't seen him for two years, and was shocked that his flaming red hair was sprinkled with gray. His body seemed to have shrunken, become more delicate.

Maria, too, had aged with the years. But in a different way. Though her hair was streaked with white and her face lined with the troubles of her lifetime, there was a serenity in her that was soothing.

"Like wine," Cesare had teased the last time Gianna was home. "Your mother, she gets better with age."

There was Julio, slender still, wearing glasses, his dark hair thinning at the temples. And Valerie, slim and elegant, her blonde hair beautifully coiffed.

Paolo was so tanned he looked like the Indians with whom he worked, but the years of hot desert sun had lightened his dark hair to almost a golden brown.

Rose was strong and matronly, heavier after so many children, full bosomed and big hipped. Mario had become a little paunchy from Rose's good cooking.

Annamarie, watching Cesare, was smiling. She was thinner—Gianna knew from her letters that life at the mission had often been hard. But when her sister turned to speak to Christopher, Gianna saw the same expression of love that had been there so long ago.

All around Cesare and Maria the grandchildren played, but there was only one who would carry the family name, Julio's red-haired son, Cesare Dellesanto the second.

Three blond, blue-eyed boys ran to Cesare, tugged at his hand. "Grandpa, Grandpa," the oldest of the Brannings begged. "Tell us how you used to make the wine."

Gianna's heart overflowed with love for her family. Oh, God, she thought, please let these children have the same beautiful dreams we had in growing up.

Her father saw her then. He rose from the bench, a child by each hand, the sunlight warm in his thick hair. There was the same smile, the old love and joy as he called to her, "Gianna! Gianna mia!"